Vivien Jones (nee Hackney) grew up in Goldenhill, Stoke-on-Trent, Staffordshire, England and graduated as a mature student from Manchester Metropolitan University.

PROLOGUE

It was one of those mornings when dewdrops cling to cobwebs and droplets of mist glisten underfoot. A day when clouds linger, shrouding the way ahead. On such a day, four strangers, detained in hospital by an unrelenting fog, face spectres from their past, which shape their futures.

THE DISCHARGE LOUNGE

VIVIEN JONES

CHAPTER ONE

"Another day, another dollar, that's what they say, don't they?" the young porter asked the somewhat flustered, receptionist as he parked a stretcher in the hospital's discharge lounge. "That's it, my dear, now don't move a muscle, Unit Number D45362, Sarah Worth," he said, checking the patient's identity bracelet. "I'll book you in with the lovely Miss Woodridge and she will sort everything out for you," he said, scooping her case notes up off the trolley.

"Thank you. You are all so kind," Sarah, said.

"Here's another one for you, Miss Woodridge," he said. Continuing to play the game and pushing his luck a little, hovering over the reception desk. "Just wondering, what time you finish? Clock-off, I mean."

"You know as well as I do, Stan, that we are on call, twenty-four-seven in this department, but if there is nothing last minute, I hope to finish by six. Twelve-hours is enough for any soul in here," she said, scanning the room. "And you, Stanley Johnson, are welcome to call me Josie - when no one is within earshot, of course!" Stan smirked. He enjoyed playing the game.

"Many on the list, Josie? In addition to Sarah Worth, this rather nice lady, of course," he added, nodding towards the stretcher and placing the patient's case notes into the 'Awaiting Discharge' tray.

"Let's see. Sarah Worth, the rather nice lady over there, makes four. I must say, Fred, that it is really considerate of you to refer to our patients by name. We are all more than the numbers used to identify us, especially in here. Anyway, up to press, there's four discharges today, five, if we include the baby. Not too bad. I've had far busier days," Josie said, glancing at the computer screen and adding Mrs Worth onto the list.

"Anyone would think we're bloody invisible," a dishevelled man, perched on the edge of a chair in the corner of the room, said. "That's it, keep wheeling them in." he added, nodding towards Sarah. The porter and receptionist both ignored him.

"Are you doing anything special after you've finished?" Stan asked, leaning over the reception desk in an attempt to lighten the situation.

"Nothing you would be interested in, Stanley," Josie said, with rather a wry smile.

"Well, you are quite mistaken about that, Miss Josie Woodridge. I would be very interested in anything and everything you will be doing tonight. Tell you what, why don't I catch up with you later? You will probably be ready for a drink or two after sorting these out, especially that one over there," he said, nodding towards the irate man. "Sounds like he can be a bit aggressive. No doubt he'll get his comeuppance one way or another. Perhaps sort him out first, if you can."

"Mmm... well, you know what they say, Stanley, there is all sorts in a box of liquorice and we are not here to judge anyone. Hospitals can be scary places at the best of times and, if you don't mind, the gentleman's name is Frederick, Frederick Rindheart. Thing is, Stanley, every patient, including these four, have a story to tell and, unfortunately, we don't have the time to listen to what they need to tell us."

The porter, having courteously been put in his place, decided to make for the door. "You are right, Josie, we are good at treating what we can see, the physical side of things, but there is so much more to us. It would be really interesting to get to know our patients and find time to listen to their stories," he said.

"Hold on a minute, Stan," she called, after him. "Perhaps I will join you for a drink and a debrief after work tonight, providing this fog lifts. It's a proper peasouper out there. In fact, I don't mind working on days like these, it's so miserable. Mind you, I don't like fog at the best of times. It clings to you. I prefer to see what's ahead of me and where I'm going. And, I don't mind telling you, that there are different types of fog. There's radiation fog, advection fog, valley fog and freezing fog, to name a few. I bet you didn't know that, did you, Stanley Johnson? And, this dense one is bringing everything to a standstill. Anyway, I'd better get on. Look forward to seeing you later, unless I get a better offer in the meantime," she teased.

Stan raised his hand and grinned. His hard to resist smile was a light in dark places and brightened the hearts of everyone it captivated. He had been sweet on Josie for a long time and if everything went to plan, their date would become a turning point in both of their lives. Working in the hospital made them all too aware that the sands of time did not stand still for prince nor pauper, which left them longing for something substantial to cling to. Life, in the health service, often felt fragile, without purpose, leaving them hungry for stability and security. They had both been secretly hoping that their relationship would blossom and fulfil their longing to be loved, yet neither of them had the courage to express their feelings, for fear of rejection. Perhaps now was the day they had both been waiting for.

"Did you hear that weather update, on the radio? You can bet the motorway is at a standstill, again," Frederick, the troublemaker, said, looking towards a well-dressed lady, sitting on a large, blue hospital chair. "Looks like we'll have a long wait in this place," he said, pacing the floor. "I don't like being couped up. It's time to get my backside out of here. Anyone else fancy doing a runner down the A34 with me?"

"Please get down off your high-horse, Frederick," the well-dressed, elderly lady, said. "You, good sir, and the patient on the trolley over there, have only just arrived. May I suggest we maintain an orderly disposition and that you, Frederick Rindheart, politely wait your turn. And, kindly afford me the decency of addressing me as Mrs Smithson," she said, wafting her discharge papers in the air.

"Well, they do say age before beauty, don't they? Madame Smithson!"

"I beg your pardon, young man! What did you say? Please refrain from mumbling!" she said, tapping her hearing aid.

"Nothing. I didn't say anything, well, nothing to shout about, if you catch my drift, Madame. Mind you, if I'm honest, I don't know what we would do without this hospital and the angels who work here, do you?" he added, nodding towards Josie whose eyes, if not her ears, were glued to the computer screen. "Anyway, how long have you been waiting in 'ere for, an' where do you come from, Madame Smithson? Go on, tell us a bit about yourself."

"Do not be so impertinent, young man. In fact, you are downright rude and far too personal and presumptuous for my liking. One hopes that you will not take umbrage if I choose to address you as Frederick. That is your Christian name, isn't it, and one which has slightly more decorum than Fred?"

"Only my mother, God rest her soul, ever called me Frederick and that was usually when she was annoyed with me after I'd been up to no good," he quipped. "But I don't mind if you use my full name since you are old enough to be my mother!"

"Unbelievably impertinent! Not an ounce of decency. One regularly wonders if all of society's dregs have been dragged up. No etiquette and certainly little respect for their betters. Unfortunately, I have little choice other than to wait in line with you and, no doubt, more of your ilk. An exclusive lounge, for the more refined members of society awaiting discharge, would be far preferable to this and would undoubtedly separate the sheep from the goats. Dragged up!" she said, looking Fred up-and-down.

"I'll have you know, Madame Smithson, that I had a mother who was worth her weight in gold and you and your sort aren't fit to have tied her shoelaces," he said, striding towards her. "And, I'll also have you know that she was worth ten of you!" he said, wagging his finger in her face.

"Please do not raise your voice or you will disturb my little one. Rather let us agree to disagree," Clarissa, a young mother, cradling her new-born son, said, attempting to diffuse the escalating situation. "We could be waiting in here for hours," she added, gazing through the huge floor to ceiling window at the ever-thickening fog, engulfing them. She pulled her son closer and whispered, "every time my heart beats it beats with love for you," and wrapped his white, crocheted shawl, around him.

"Hear, hear. Well said, young lady," Sarah, the patient who had just arrived on the trolley, said, sitting upright to make her point. "The last thing we want, given the circumstances, is unpleasant discord. We need to demonstrate patience and understanding in this difficult situation. Besides, we do not want to disturb the baby and, you are right, we could be delayed indefinitely if this fog doesn't lift soon. Does anyone know when the next train to London, Euston is due? I am all packed and ready to go," she added, scanning the room.

Disregarding Sarah's unusual request for information about trains and timetables, Madame Smithson said, "manners are so hard to find these days and there is certainly a lack of respect for the elderly. Still, where there is very little sense there is said to be very little feeling. Thank goodness, my son will be collecting me soon," she declared, standing to her feet and peering through the window. "Then again, he is a very important man, at the pinnacle of his MI6 career in the secret intelligence service. One is obviously extremely proud of him, but time is always of the essence and I must be ready to fly whenever he arrives. It is normally a very quick turnround," she said, buttoning-up her coat. "He will not have a minute to spare. I must be ready."

"Son, did you say? You have a son, Madame Smithson?" Frederick asked.

"I do, young man, not that that it is any of your business!"

"Well, can I get anyone a drink?" Fred asked, hoping to pour a little oil on troubled waters. "Waiting around is thirsty work and looking at this peasouper it's unlikely that any of us will be going anywhere for quite some time. We are well and truly stuck with each other so let's not make waves, shall we? Pity there isn't a bar, though."

Josie glanced over the top of her computer screen, scanning the waiting area. "That's right," she said. "All present and correct. I just need to doublecheck the paperwork and tick you all off on my list. Frederick Rindheart; Penelope Smithson; Sarah Worth; Clarissa Noble and child," she said, nodding at each of them as she did so.

11

Penelope Smithson or Madame Smithson to Fred, buttoned and unbuttoned her coat again as she walked towards the picture window to search the swirling fog.

"Look, look," she called out, quite out of character for one so refined. "It's a little girl, isn't it, with ringlets and ribbons in her hair? There in the middle of that dense patch of fog. Can anyone else see her? Frederick, can *you* see her?"

"All I can see is fog and if you can see anything else out there then you need to get your eyes tested, Madame Smithson," he replied, squinting at the mist. "Sit yourself down and stop fretting. I'll keep a lookout for that son of yours. What will he be driving? A Rolls Royce, no doubt!"

Penelope Smithson did not answer Fred. Dumbfounded, she unbuttoned her coat again and sat back down, in no doubt whatsoever about the identity of the little girl she had seen in the fog engulfing them. Melancholia almost overwhelmed her, wrapping itself around her, tighter than the coat she was wearing, suffocating her and threatening to extinguish every ounce of hope she possessed. Subdued and alone with her memories of a past life, she regressed. Was there to be no permanent escape from the sorrows of the past and why here, why now? She had successfully suppressed and controlled her recollections for the majority of her life and was an expert at ignoring their taunts. She would not allow them to resurface and overtake her. Not here, not now, never.

Fred stood, motionless, staring through the huge window into the dense, swirling fog. He was no longer searching for a young girl or Madame's son. What he saw in the fog, what demanded his attention and mesmerised him, was a distressing image from his own past. For all his bravado, a cold shiver travelled straight down the middle of his spine. He wanted to look away and hide his face but a power beyond his own would not allow him to do so. Slumping into the nearest chair he buried his head in his hands and muttered: "Not now, please, not now." But it was too late, far too late. He watched, glued to his boyhood images.

CHAPTER TWO

"Frederick! Where are you and what are you up to?" Kathleen, his mother shouted over the backyard gate.

"Up to no-good again; no doubt!" she said. "At twelve years old, he should know better. I just hope there's not too much of his father in him or he will end up on the wrong side of law. Nothing so sure. At least he has stopped playing with wooden swords and bows and arrows. Why he has to win at everything though, I will never know. It's a wonder he hasn't put someone's eye out before now, he's that roughshod," his mother muttered, as she pegged washing along the clothesline, in a small backyard, in the village of Goldendale.

"Better fill up the paraffin lamp in the lavatory next and cut-up last night's 'Evening Sentinel' to put on the nail on the back of the door. I have no idea how Fred gets through so much newspaper. Perhaps he reads it first. He's in there long enough."

"I've finished the cart, lads! We are in for the ride of our lives," Fred, the ringleader, called to a group of boys as he yanked at a rope in an attempt to steer his latest creation down the street.

"Bumper cars and fairground rides will have nothing on 'Silver' here. Hope you lot have finished making our Guy

Fawkes. We've got plenty of fetching and carrying to do and 'Silver' here will help us make light work of it. She's a beauty, isn't she?"

Every member of his motley gang gathered around him to inspect his latest creation, all nodding their approval. Having recently found a discarded baby's pram on the local banks, the rubbish heap, to be precise, Fred made a go-cart, of sorts, from its dismembered parts. Its large wheels, chassis and frame were ideal and a length of rope tied to the front of it, became a makeshift, crude, steering mechanism. The only piece of equipment missing was a brake pedal but, then again, Fred would never succumb to needing or using one of those.

It was towards the end of October, almost bonfire night. The boys, under Fred's leadership, had been busy collecting firewood and pieces of old furniture, not to mention having had several attempts at making a realistic 'Guy Fawkes'. After stuffing newspapers into the legs and arms of a pair of trousers and jumper, which had both seen better days, they tied it all together with string and attempted to create an oval-shaped face mask from a piece of cardboard. Unfortunately, a scarecrow-like monstrosity was the result of their best efforts and a far-cry from anything close to an effigy of 'Guy Fawkes'.

"We'll never get any money for that thing," Sam, one of the motley crew, confidently declared. "And you know what that means, don't you? We'll not be able to buy any fireworks, especially penny bangers!"

Sam was right. No passer-by would look twice at their Guy, let alone put their hands into their pockets to donate their loose change. Rivalry between the numerous groups of young boys in the village was rife and winning every clash of the titans was paramount. Which group had the best 'Guy Fawkes' on top of the biggest bonfire was one of their annual competitions and one which Fred, and his band of brothers, had to win. As the big day loomed, some of the boys stood guard day and night to protect their group's plunder. It was not unknown for old tyres, settees and chairs to go missing overnight from one pyre and miraculously appear on a rival gang's bonfire the following morning, even 'Guys' had been known to disappear. Pride, if nothing else, was at stake on the run-up to the big night and Fred was determined not be outdone. Inspecting their feeble creation of a Guy Fawkes, Fred had one of his brilliant brainwaves.

"I know," he said. "We'll dress-up young Billy 'ere as our guy and wheel him onto the High Street sitting on 'Silver', over there!"

"I don't want to be a Guy," young Billy cried, panic engulfing him. "I know what happens to Guys on bonfire night and I don't want to be one."

"Don't be so daft and stop whinging. You'll only have to pretend to be one until we get enough money to buy some bangers and, if you want to tag along with us and be in our gang, then you will have to do it. Now wipe your nose and put these old clothes on over the top of your own. Be quick about it. My Dad told me, before he was sent down, that time is money and we haven't got all day, so get on with it. That's it. Now cover yourself with this mud, stick some straw out of the top of your coat, put this mask on and pull that big, old cap down over your face. Wow! I

16

think we're onto a winner, Billy-boy!" Fred said, standing back to admire his creation. Members of the gang took it in turns to adjust the living, breathing, image of 'Guy Fawkes'. Billy had little choice other than to play his part, especially if he wanted to become a bone fide member of the best gang on the Hill.

"Right, get yourself comfy on Silver, and play dead, Billy. That's one thing you are good at doing, so don't you dare let us down or we won't let you tag along with us anymore."

Fred, as usual, took the lead and pulled the trolley into the High Street, parking it outside 'The Wheatsheaf' public house. It was Saturday morning and the road was buzzing. Trade was good and if Billy played his part convincingly they would be buying catherine wheels, rockets and a bag full of penny bangers before the day was done.

"Spare a copper for the guy, mister?" Fred, boldly said, accosting the first passer-by, but to no avail. Not one to be defeated, he persevered. "Please can you spare a copper for the guy, mister?" Adding manners worked wonders, just as his mother said it would. She regularly recited 'manners maketh a man' to him, but it was something Fred didn't understand nor take a blind bit of notice of, nevertheless, in this instance, it worked.

The well-dressed man didn't give Billy a second look but threw some coppers onto the floor. Fred scooped them up.

"Our first bangers," he said, triumphantly. "Keep up the good work, Billy. You'll turn out to be a little gold mine."

"But, I'm hungry and I need the loo. I'm bursting for a pee," Billy muttered.

"Shut up! You will have to hold it in for a bit longer and keep your mouth shut. We're on a roll and you are going nowhere."

Fred's gang was on target for a bumper day until Terry, the leader of a rival gang, crossed the road to take a closer look at their realistic 'Guy Fawkes'. He didn't need to look twice at it and gave Silver, and the Guy sitting precariously on top of it, a massive kick. Billy shouted out in pain and gripped his leg. The game was up and Terry lost no time in publicly declaring the truth of the matter to the captive audience, resulting in reactions of disgust and amusement, from the onlookers.

"We will get you back for this an' keep your thieving hands off our takings and our bonfire," Fred said, squaring up to Terry. One look, one threat from Fred was enough. Terry backed down. No one messed with Fred; no one ever would.

*****

"Are you quite well, Frederick?" Madame Smithson, asked, tentatively placing her hand on his back.

"Me? I'm as fit as a flea, Madame. Don't be concerning yourself about me. I am sure you've got more important things on your mind. Anyway, where's that son of yours? What time are you expecting him?"

18

"I have absolutely no idea. Surely, it will depend on the weather conditions. But, whatever time he arrives I will be ready and waiting for him. He is a very busy man."

"I'm sure he is. Sounds like he's too busy for his old mum! Doesn't know what side his bread is buttered on, if you ask me."

"I am not asking you Frederick and I would be extremely grateful if you would kindly keep your misplaced conceptions to yourself. I was merely enquiring after your welfare since you looked perturbed, that is all. In fact, I was about to relay my concerns to the receptionist when you straightened up a little."

"Don't be getting your knickers in a twist about me, your ladyship. I'm as right as ninepence. Your time would be better spent minding yourself with your own business and placing a bet on when that son of yours might show his face. It's like waiting for Christmas and I bet there's more chance of you being hit by lightning than him showing up here!"

Penelope Smithson refused to acknowledge Fred's retorts but stood up, straightened her back and walked towards the window.

"Is your baby still sleeping, Clarissa?" she asked, sitting down next to her.

"He's as good as gold, isn't he?" Clarissa said. "Barely makes a murmur, apart from when he's hungry, of course. He is such a blessing. We haven't decided on a name for

19

him yet, although I would like to name him after my grandfather, Archibald, Archie for short."

Penelope stiffened. "Think very carefully before you finally decide on a name for him, my dear. A name says so much about oneself, one's breeding and upbringing.

"Would you like to join us, over here, Sarah?" Penelope called to the patient on the trolley. "Do come and have a look at this little chap. He is so handsome."

Sarah did not need asking twice and gingerly walked across the waiting area and sat down next to Clarissa. "He is very handsome, isn't he?" she said, pulling the shawl away from his button-nosed, face. "And, I am sure that you will make a wonderful mother, Clarissa. His grandmother must be bursting with pride. A new life and new beginnings bring hope to all of us and there is nothing quite like a new born child to do just that. Precious they are, treasures in their own uniqueness. Not that it is something I have had the privilege and pleasure of experiencing myself, but they are treasures nonetheless and I envy your mother, baby's grandmother."

Clarissa pulled the shawl back over her little one's face. "I don't really know where my Mother is now," she calmly said. "But I do hope, wherever she is, that she knows that I have had a baby and that she has a grandson. She must know."

An uncomfortable hush fell like a weighted cloud over the three women and the unnamed child. How could a mother not know that her daughter had given birth to a son? Clarissa knew the answer and was living with the consequences of it. The mention of her own mother caused her to reminisce as pictures of her own past started to form in the thickening fog surrounding them.

CHAPTER THREE

"Clarissa, where on earth are you going dressed like that? You look like something the cat's dragged in?" Violet, her mother, asked.

"Nowhere special, mum. Just out and about. I'm meeting a few friends in the coffee shop down town, if that's ok with the police. There isn't a law against that now, is there? Afterall, I am seventeen not seven. I'm not your little girl anymore so please, do me a favour, and stop treating me like one. Francis goes wherever she wants to, whenever she wants to and is of the opinion that your hold over me is too tight. She says I'm tied to your apron strings."

"I am not interested in where Francis goes or what Francis does and I'm certainly not interested in any opinion she may hold about me or anyone else. You'll see where she will end up! And, you can tell Francis that we have big plans for you, my girl, not that it is any of her business. You've got a good head on your shoulders, Clarissa, and your father and I are going to make damn sure you put it to good use. The sky's the limit, if you play your cards right. All you have to do is focus on your exam grades and secure your place at university. You will be the first one of our family to walk down Keele's hallowed halls. And, while I'm at it, your dad won't be impressed if he sees the length of that skirt. Half way up your backside it is."

"Don't worry mum. Dad won't see it and I do know right from wrong. I should do. I've had it pushed down my throat since the day I could put one foot in front of the other. Please get off my case and give me a break. It isn't too much to ask, is it? I've done my UCAS application and my projected grades will definitely secure me a place at Uni. Don't worry. I won't let you down. I know how much it means to you both."

"I know you won't. It's just that when I was growing up, university was beyond the reach of working-class folk, like me, especially women. I wish I'd had half the chances you've got. In my day, if you didn't pass your eleven-plus, assuming you had been entered for it, you were earmarked for everything other than university. Anything marked academic was ruled out of the curriculum and the doors marked 'Degree' and 'Professional Career' were firmly locked to the less educated, less privileged and less fortunate. I swear my secondary school education was designed to make me into a perfect wife and mother! And, if I'm honest, I never enjoyed needlework nor cookery classes. I did learn how to prepare a tea-tray though, which comes in handy when I'm serving afternoon tea to your dad! What I did want to study was biology and science and English literature and..."

"Oh! give it a rest, Mum. I've heard all this before. Boring!"

"Give it a rest! Give you a break! I'll give you what for if you are not back in this house by ten o'clock, young lady. You don't realise or appreciate how fortunate you are."

"Make it ten-thirty and we've got a deal."

"You cheeky monkey. I said ten o'clock and ten o'clock it is unless you want your father turning up outside the coffee shop."

"Ten o'clock it is then, mum, but not a minute before and tell dad that I can find my own way home and I'll be in the house before the clock, over there, strikes ten. May as well call me Cinderella! Well not really, because Cinderella got to stay out until the clock struck midnight. One thing's for sure, I will definitely be living in the halls of residence this time next year and I'll stay out dancing 'til I'm too tired to put one foot in front of the other. No more lights out and in bed by ten for me! That's what university life is all about, having a good time. Bring it on! The sooner the better," she said, disappearing through the back door.

Violet sunk into a cosy armchair in the corner of the room, her carefree daughter slamming the front door behind her. The house felt empty, bereft, without Clarissa and, in robotic mode, Violet decided to clean the kitchen table before making a meat-and-potato pie for tea. Perhaps some of her secondary school education was being put to good use, after all. She had managed to create a homely, warm and safe place to live out of a next-to-nothing income and yet, next-to-nothing was far more than her own parents had lived on. Although content with her lot, she could not resist wondering what she may have become, had opportunity, at eleven years of age, shone its light on her path more brightly. Perhaps it was her English essay which had let her down and stamped 'fail' on her examination papers, assigning her to the local secondary modern girls' school. Despite her initial disappointment, Violet's school years had been happy, if limiting, ones. Having left school at fifteen, without a qualification to her name and, as the eldest of a big family, she finished her school years on a Friday afternoon in July and clocked-on for her first shift in a local pot bank the following Monday morning. At the end of her second working week, having worked a week in hand, she turned the entire contents of her wage packet over to her mother to boost their family's income. A meagre amount of pocket-money, returned to her as a treat, did not stretch very far and anything classed as a luxury was strictly off-limits, beyond her reach and expectations. Her interest in anatomy and biology would surely, given the right conditions and a favourable wind, have secured her a career in nursing. But such was the disparity of the age and times that unreachable stars remained just that for the vast majority of working-class society. Violet yearned for a fairer playing field, not solely for Clarissa, but society as a whole. One way or another she would do all in her power to create, nurture and maximise her daughter's opportunities and prospects. Regardless of the cost, she would do all in her power to ensure that no star was unreachable for her child.

Clarissa almost ran, not into the coffee shop, but straight into The Swan, a local pub. Despite being under age, she looked much older than her years, and had recently discovered that she preferred the atmosphere of the pub to that of the coffee shop and the taste of cider to that of coffee. A small group of young men, the local talent, gathered around the jukebox. Pop songs floated on the billows of cigarette smoke in the tiny, snug area. She loved too many of the songs and artists to have favourites and sang along to the majority of them. What her parents didn't know wouldn't hurt them, would it? She glanced at her watch. She had three hours of freedom before curfew.

"Can I get you a drink?" a well-spoken, smartly dressed, young man asked. He wasn't a local lad, one born and bred in the village on the hill, but there was something surreal about him, as if they had met before. Perhaps this place, this moment in time, was meant to be.

*****

"What's going on over 'ere?" Fred asked, approaching the three women, small-talking in the discharge lounge whilst awaiting their freedom. "Bet this little chap is the attraction. What's his name?"

"We can't decide on a name. Archie is favourite, though," Clarissa said.

"Frederick is a strong name, you know. Someone once told me that it has leadership qualities."

"I didn't know you were a comedian, Frederick," Penelope, said. "I have already informed Clarissa that she must take great care when deciding on a name for this young man. I am confident, however, that *Fred* in any format is totally unsuitable. Leadership qualities, indeed!"

"I'll have you know, Madame Smithson, that I had my share of fun as a boy and was the leader of the local pack. No one messed with me," he said.

26

CHAPTER FOUR

Fred ensured that bonfire night finally arrived without too many squabbles, scrapes and fisticuffs. Silver proved her worth in gold and Fred and his band of brothers won both the village green bonfire and firework display, hands down. One of the local newsagents, who had been both amused and impressed by the initiative Fred had demonstrated in the creation of a Guy Fawkes, decided to employ him to deliver his papers. Fred rose to the challenge and, because he was paid a lump sum to divide between his gang, he quickly drew up a rota. Silver was being used more now, to deliver the news, than she had ever been to cradle a baby. Daily newspapers were piled on top of her after being divided into streets and tied into bundles with frayed pieces of string. The customer's house number was pencilled on the top corner of each paper. It was easy money. Silver's wheels never stopped turning and young Billy was prepared to run his legs off for less payment than any of the older boys. Needless to say, Billy soon hogged the top-spot on Fred's rota and was his first port of call for every shift. It was Billy's job to neatly push the newspapers through the corresponding letterboxes. He had found his first niche in life and the fact that he was paid less than any of his peers for his hard labour never entered the equation. Billy relished the opportunity, was a quick learner and, almost overnight, became Fred's right-hand man. Due to the lucrative financial arrangement, Fred quickly amassed enough money to fulfil the first of his many ambitions. He bought himself a bicycle. It wasn't a new bicycle, but it was his and, inadvertently, he became the proud owner of a fleet of two vehicles! 'Faithful Silver' and 'Fearless Samson' were his pride and joy and one of his boy-hood claims to fame.

Early the following morning, after cleaning and polishing his latest acquisition and before anyone was out of bed, Fred rode Samson, on her maiden voyage, up and down the wide entry, behind the long row of terraces. It would never do to be seen falling off his bike, so he minimised the risk by carefully swerving in and out of the cobblestones. Fred need not have feared humiliation, falling nor failure. He was a born natural and liked to think he took to riding a bike as well, if not better than, any professional. Before the end of the day, he was seen competently riding his Samson, over every inch of the hill. Later that night, he firmly fastened the top button of his navy-blue coat and freewheeled down Gill Bank Lane, one of the steepest inclines on the Hill. His cap blew away and his coat splayed out forming a cape behind him. He let go of the handlebars and put both his arms into the air. He was a super hero. His destiny defined.

*****

"Now then, Madame Smithson, perhaps you would be kind enough to tell us what name *you* think is suitable for this little chap," Frederick said, looking down at Clarissa's sleeping babe. "Because, in my book, Archie or Archibald and Fred or Frederick, are both, strong, admirable names.

"My son's name is Edward which is an old English name steeped with fortune and wealth. Fortune and wealth have certainly been evident throughout his life, particularly

28

during his career with MI6. His name does have other connotations, of course, but I cannot bring them to mind at the moment. Fortune and wealth are the predominate factors though and are most certainly life's most important ones."

"Silver spoon syndrome, if you ask me, Madame," Fred said. "Life's the luck of the draw in more ways than one and it sounds to me as though your son was born into wealth rather than earning it. Diamonds handed to him, served on a silver platter. Bet you've got more money than soft Mick!"

Penelope ignored his comments.

"My mother was poor," Clarissa said, "but she insisted that being born into poverty was the making of her. She told me that her character had been forged in the fires of depravation. Strange that. I would have thought that poverty would have been her downfall had I not seen her tenacity for myself. What do you think, Sarah? You've been very quiet since joining us. Are you ok?"

"Yes, I'm fine, truly I am. I was just daydreaming about my own life. Family are like jewels in life's crown, aren't they? Jewels, which although not finely honed, are jewels nonetheless and their uniqueness makes them priceless, irreplaceable treasures. I just wish that I had been blessed with children of my own. You are so very fortunate, Clarissa."

Before any of them could respond to Sarah's comments, the door to the waiting room opened and Stan, the porter, brazenly strolled over to the reception desk.

"Are any of these causing you trouble, Josie?" he said, making idle conversation, whilst scanning the room.

"None whatsoever, Stanley. In fact, it has been extremely quiet and no one has complained up to press, but you will be the first to hear about it if any of them do! Anyway, what are you up to? Are you on a break?"

"I was passing and since I have a few minutes to spare I thought I would check to see how you are coping. I've been at a bit of a loose-end today. Hope our get-together is still on the cards for later, though?"

"Well, if I'm honest, I could do with a drink and a catch-up now so, yes, it's definitely still on my agenda, providing there are no last-minute discharges. The fog's not budging much though, is it?"

"Still thick and murky out there," he said, looking over the top of the patients and glancing through the huge window. "It's caused a few accidents. A&E is packed out and the local roads are chock-a-block. Fingers crossed it will have cleared before you get off duty and these four, five counting the little one, will have all been sent packing. Would you like anything from the canteen? I'll be heading there in half-an-hour or so," he said, glancing at his watch and playing the game to perfection.

"I've got something to eat, thanks, and there's plenty of drinks in the machine. It was filled up this morning. Appreciate your offer though but I'm saving myself for a couple of drinks and a debrief later."

"No problem. I'll pop in again this afternoon, just to update you on the situation."

"I'd better crack-on, Stanley. I've almost finished the transfers. Just need to double-check the documentation. I don't want any eleventh-hour hold ups. Thanks again for calling-in. Look forward to seeing you later."

"Did you hear all that?" Fred said. "Wonder what he's after. More than a drink, you can bet!"

"Do not be so uncouth! I find you extremely crude, Frederick," Penelope, said.

"Well, haven't you been young yourself once, Madame? Best time of your life it is and that porter obviously thinks he's on a promise."

"I beg to differ with that statement; about being young, I mean," Clarissa, said. "I hope that how I feel now isn't going to turn out to be the best time of my life! Then again, this little one has brought so much joy with him into the world and I am grateful to him for that much. But, life has been hard, difficult for me to come to terms with."

"Well, I don't know if that statement about children is true, either," Fred, said. "I don't think for one minute that every child born into this world brings joy with it. You know what they say, if you've got none to laugh with, you've got none to cry over."

"I do not believe that, Fred. Every child is a gift, a blessing but, sadly, many of us, like me, underestimate our mother's love for us until it's too late," Clarissa said, looking at her own baby's contented face.

Sensing he was outnumbered, again, Fred walked over to the window. "No sign of Master Edward yet, Madame Smithson."

"Did you not hear what the porter said, Frederick? Traffic is at a standstill. No doubt, my son has been delayed but I remain confident that he will arrive soon," she said, standing up to fasten her coat.

Penelope did not join Fred at the window and ignored her inclination to glance at the fog again for fear of catching a glimpse of the little girl, the one she had recognised, the one with ringlets and ribbons in her hair.

CHAPTER FIVE

Overcome with fatigue, Penelope closed her heavy eyes and fell asleep in a reclining chair, in the corner of the discharge lounge. But, it was not to be a sleep of slumbers awaiting her, but one of fitful memories, the worst of nightmares.

Frederick had been wrong in his assumptions. Penelope vividly remembered being young and the joy and freedom it afforded her. Yes, it was true, she had been privileged, even spoilt in many respects, but that was a truth which only enhanced the wealth of experiences she enjoyed, unbridled fun and the very best of happy, carefree, childhoods. A childhood which overflowed with fun and laughter, until, one day, quite unexpectedly, her world was turned upside down. A day on which everything changed.

It was a beautiful, hot, humid afternoon in the middle of June. Penelope had been busy practising croquet on the lawn of the family's sprawling estate; a lawn surrounded by huge oaks and giant pots of bright-red geraniums. Greek goddesses, ornate stone planters, fragrant rose gardens and arched trellises, draped with wisteria, contributed to the utopian surroundings. The focal point of the garden was, without doubt, the huge tiered fountain, fashioned on Sir Charles Barry's famous fountains in Trafalgar Square. The bottom tier of the masterpiece formed a pond deep enough for giant koi carp to wallow and prosper in. Life was perfect, simply perfect.

Penelope had first tried her hand at croquet with a small group of select friends at her ninth birthday party in August, the year before. The game complimented the homemade, tarty lemonade, sponge cakes, smothered in lemon icing, filled with buttercream and topped-off with a fresh cherry. Cook had pulled out all the stops to make her birthday as special as possible, since her parents, due to an appointment in London, were unable to share in her birthday treats.

Penelope liked to win at everything she played. In fact, she had to win at everything, and although she had won every game at her birthday party, she realised that her guests had been dutybound to ensure her victory in everything they played. No longer content with winning by default, she determined to master her ability to hit the coloured balls expertly through the appropriate hoops; her aim and score was, at long last, improving with every swing of the mallet.

"Please come inside Miss Penelope," nanny, called.

"Not yet, nanny. Not while I'm winning!"

"Winning! How can you possibly be winning? You are not playing against anyone therefore you cannot lose. Come along now," nanny said, reaching for her hand. "Perhaps your imaginary opponents will continue the game with you later, although I have no doubt who will be the winner!"

"But, I don't want to go in! I want to play. Here you are, you can play with me, nanny. You can be my opponent," she said, hurling a mallet towards her and brushing her calf as it flew past her."

"I have no time to play games with you or anyone else, young lady, and please do not throw things into the air. Your mother and father have asked to see you and see you they will. Now come along, nicely," she said, smoothing down her navy-blue uniform and readjusting her white apron. "They have travelled all the way from London to see you."

"One does not *have* to do everything one is instructed to do, nanny! Why have I got to go inside anyway? Please do not spoil my fun."

"Well, if you must know, Miss, your parents have a rather nice surprise for you," she said, stooping down and looking straight into her big, brown eyes.

"Another surprise!" she screamed, clapping her hands. "I must say, that I was *very* upset not to receive a pony for my birthday. I am almost ten now and poppa promised me that I would definitely have a pony of my own when I was old enough. Ten is quite old enough. My poppa and step-momma both own a horse and there is plenty of room in the stables for another one. I will call him Champion. Come along, Nanny! What are you waiting for, silly billy? I love surprises and this one will have four legs, a saddle and a set of reins. I *must* have a riding crop, as well, though. Champion and I are going to win lots of races and first-place prizes. Come on, Nanny. Don't be such a slow coach. One never wins a prize for lagging behind."

*****

Penelope stirred and opened her eyes, only to see Frederick standing guard over her.

"Just checking you're still breathing, Madame. At least you are in the best place if you decide to pop your clogs, though. Mind you, I don't blame you for trying to get some shuteye. What else is there to do in 'ere and no doubt that son of yours, Edward, did you say his name was, will not be arriving anytime soon? The fog looks worse than ever out there."

"Edward will arrive as soon as he is able to. He will not be deterred in any mission."

"Let's hope he is prepared to move heaven and earth to get here then. That fog's not budging an inch," he said, peering out of the window for the umpteenth time.

Sarah, rather timidly, stood to her feet and joined Fred in scanning the thickening fog, looking for a glimmer of light through the eeriness and intimidation it was creating.

"I'll put a bit of music on. It may brighten this place up while we are all waiting for the fog to clear," Josie, the receptionist, said, tuning-in to 'Radio Stoke'. But, the weather forecast continued to sound gloomy and the sounds of the latest hits did little to lift the spirits of those waiting to escape.

"I must sit down," Sarah, said. "My legs aren't as young as they used to be and I do not care to look upon what might have been, what I could have, or should have done,

36

to have changed the trajectory of my life. It boils down to what a lot of people, from all walks of life, spout about these days: 'it is what it is, not what it should have been or could have been, but it is what it is!'"

"Have *you* seen something unpleasant out there, in the fog, as well, Sarah?" Fred, asked, not having mentioned his own, uncanny, experience.

"I prefer not to talk about it. Besides, what I thought I saw outside, in the mist, happened a long time ago, in another life, to be precise. A life that was mine for the taking but one which I allowed to pass me by," Sarah said.

"Leave her be," Clarissa, said, repositioning her baby boy in her arms. "I can appreciate why Sarah does not want to tell anyone what she has seen out there," she said, nodding towards the window. "Whatever it was, it is best ignored, forgotten. Fog is such a strange phenomenon. It plays tricks on us. Try to grasp or touch it if you don't believe me. It just dissipates through your fingers, rather like life, when you try to hold on to it and it evaporates before your eyes."

"It certainly does," Sarah, said. "And, if I'm honest, my life has felt foggy for a long time. Nothing I have done, apart from working as a stenographer during the war years, has amounted to much. Missed opportunities and the life they offered evaporated with every one of my hopes and ambitions, a bit like the mist surrounding us now. Sometimes, it is the things we do not do, the opportunities we do not grasp, which surface to haunt us. Unfortunately, there is no going back. No rewind or replay button. We live, as best we can, with the consequences of our choices, mulling over its leftovers alongside the strands of what might have been."

"Is someone coming to collect you, Sarah? To take you home?" Clarissa asked.

"Someone will definitely come for me, although I am unsure who that someone will be," Sarah said. "I wish I could remember but, then again, perhaps it is a kindness that we forget some of life's trials and tribulations, don't you think? Does anyone know when the next train to London Euston is due? I am packed up and ready to go." No one answered the question Sarah continued to pose, recognising the sadness it represented.

"Please will you turn that radio up a bit and find something light-hearted?" Fred, called to Josie, who chose to ignore his demand. "I realise that we are all getting a bit fed up of playing the waiting game, but let's change our tune and be a bit more upbeat, shall we? Afterall, we've had our discharge papers and we will be getting out of here as soon as the fog lifts so let's not lose our rag. We just need to be patient patients, if you'll pardon the pun! Then again, if you had seen half the things I've witnessed you would be more appreciative of our situation, even thankful for it. I remember the day my life took a very important turn.

CHAPTER SIX

"Explain it to me again, Frederick. Why are you and Billy enlisting in the army?" his mother, asked.

"Because there is nothing for us round 'ere, mam, only dead-end jobs."

"Well, you are safer down the pit than in the army and that's all I'm bothered about, your safety."

"You know full well that I couldn't stomach the pit, don't you, mam? Can you remember the day I went down the mine on our school daytrip? Part of our career search, they dared to call it! As soon as they closed the cage and we started to drop down, I panicked. I tried not to let on how I felt to the rest of the class, though. Buttoned my lips, I did. But my heart was beating twenty to the dozen. I couldn't breathe down there. How men crawl along those narrow tunnels in the filth and dark, I will never know. Earn every penny, they do. Besides, what else is there for me and my mates round here, mam? At least we'll be serving our King and country in the forces and there is no greater honour than that. And, we'd rather jump in than be conscripted."

"You are right, son, there isn't any honour greater than that, but you will not be safer in army. Somewhere along the line you will find yourself fighting your fellowman, mankind's brothers!" Fred threw his head back and laughed.

"Don't make me laugh! Safer down the pit than in the forces. Pull the other one, mam. What planet are you on? Accidents happen down the pit every day God sends. Some have lost their lives and been buried alive down there, underneath our feet, they are! So, please don't try an' tell me that I will be safer down there than serving my country. Besides, who do you think I'll be fighting if I enlist? There isn't another world war being waged, yet."

"There is always a war or rumours of wars rumbling somewhere in the world. We are never truly at peace with our neighbours. I don't want you fighting a faceless enemy in a far-off land. The thought of it is too much to bear and if anything happened to you I would…"

"Stop right there. That's enough of that talk. I will be trained-up in the army and learn lots of new skills. It won't half give me a leg up and set me up for the rest of my life. Besides, I've got Billy, who's coming with me, to think about. Looks up to me, he does. And, after we have served our time we are going to set up our own business. We've got it all planned, so stop worrying. Nothing is going to happen to me."

"You will never stop me from worrying about you. Fingers crossed, you won't be accepted for duty, Frederick. Not everyone is. There's lots of entrance tests and fitness requirements to get through first."

"I *will* be accepted, mam. I will make damn sure I am, one way or another. And, just think, I'll send you my pay and you can treat yourself to something nice for a change, and save what's left over. Seven years will fly by and I'll have a nice nest-egg waiting for me when I'm discharged.

"An awful lot can happen in seven years," she said, and she was right.

*****

"Come along, nanny. Do hurry. You can be such a slowcoach," Penelope called. "Do you think my pony, my Champion, is in our stables? Shall we make straight for there to save time? I do hope that I will have a pair of jodhpurs, a black hat and a matching red and black jacket, as well. I must look the part. Everyone, but everyone will look up to me, and so they should, but I will not allow anyone to ride my Champion. I do not have to share anything of mine with anyone else, ever."

Penelope skipped over every inch of the ground beneath her feet on their way to the ornate, entrance doors. She was at her happiest at such moments. Leaving nanny trailing behind her, she burst into the sitting room.

"Poppa, poppa! Where is Champion? I know you have bought him for me. Thank you so much."

"Calm down, Penelope. Do be quiet," Lord Cuthbertson, said. "Oh! there you are, nanny."

"Sorry, my lord, I have a job to keep pace with the little lady these days. I am not as young as I used to be!"

"Please sit down. Not there, Penelope! That's it, you can sit next to nanny on the chaise lounge while she gets her breath back. That will do nicely. Now then, whatever is all the excitement about? Who, may I ask, is Champion?"

"Do not toy with me, poppa. You know very well who Champion is."

Lord Cuthbertson glanced at nanny for a glimmer of clarification, but her lips remained sealed. She knew better than to burst lady Penelope's bubble and woe betide the unfortunate person who did.

"Champion is my pony, poppa, my very own horse, my very late birthday present. He is in the stables, isn't he? He must be. Can we go to him now? Forthwith."

Her father sighed and sat down on an armchair next to the writing bureau.

"Have you not told her, nanny? Not hinted at her surprise. The child has no inclination."

"None, your lordship."

"Come with me, Penelope," he said, taking her by the hand. "Please join us as well, nanny, assuming you have no objections, of course." Nanny had little or no choice in the matter and dutifully trailed behind them.

"Yippee! we are going to the stables. We are. We are," Penelope cried, releasing her father's grip and dancing around the drawing room.

"We are *not* going to the stables, child. Now come with me," he said, quite firmly. Father and daughter, hand-in-hand, walked towards the door, followed by nanny who was dreading the repercussions of what was about to take place. There was little doubt in her mind who would pay the price, in more ways than one, for Penelope's belated birthday surprise.

*****

Clarissa was true to her word and arrived home just as the clock was striking ten. That she was on time did not prevent her father from standing on the front step of their house, watching and waiting for her to appear. As soon as he spotted her turning the corner at the end of their street, he knew she was safe and closed the door. Clarissa had, of course, already seen him and deliberately ensured that she did not enter the house until the clock, standing proud, in the middle of the mantlepiece, had started to strike ten.

"That's a good girl," her mother, said. "Would you like me to make you a nice cup of hot cocoa?"

"Not for me, thanks, mum. I'm bursting at the seams with coffee," she said, which wasn't true. What Clarissa was bursting at the seams with was scrumpy cider, and far too much of it. Despite having downed half a packet of mints on her walk home, she was conscious that her parents may smell alcohol or cigarette smoke on her and swiftly said goodnight and made for bed, not that she would be able to sleep. Her head was pounding with the sounds of the jukebox, too much cider and Darren's words of love, which he had whispered in her ear in the entry at the back of The Swan. She had fallen in love with him and dreams of examination results, university places and travelling the world faded into insignificance in the warmth of his embrace and his passion for every inch of her. Besides,

43

what the world needed, according to the pop charts, was love, nothing more, nothing less, just love. Clarissa finally managed to fall asleep dreaming of her first boyfriend and their future together. She knew, for obvious reasons, that it would not be an easy future, but nothing was stronger than the power of love, was it?

*****

"Miss Worth, Sarah Worth, is it not?" an official, wearing a navy pin-striped suit, asked the attractive, smartly dressed, young lady, sitting behind a desk in the pool of stenographers.

"Yes, it is Sir."

"I appreciate that it is rather late in the day, but I need to dictate a last-minute letter of immense national importance. It is crucial that it makes tonight's post. Will you be able to squeeze it in, make it a priority, Miss Worth?"

"Of course, sir. No problem at all," she said, without glancing at her watch.

Sarah followed the top official into his oak-panelled, government office and respectively stood to one-side until he had taken his seat on a high-backed, black leather chair behind an oversized, solid-wood, desk. It could be described as an intimidating room due, in part, to the portraits of past officials covering its walls and who, undoubtedly, continued to look down on lesser mortals.

"Please sit down, Miss Worth," he said, taking out a pipe and refilling it with tobacco. "It helps me to concentrate, sharpens my wits," he said. Sarah smiled and

44

tried not to cough when the distinctive, addictive, aroma filled the room.

Having studied shorthand and typewriting at school, Sarah surpassed every other pupil on her way to the top of her class. Her speed and accuracy were admirable and she was, without doubt, the best of the bunch adorning the typing pool of the government office. Some of her more astute peers recognised that such popularity had its drawbacks, not least when it came to the transcription of last-minute documents and therefore never vied for the limelight, surrendering pole position to Sarah. There was no doubt in the official's mind that his letter would be perfectly presented, signed and posted that evening. Sarah's minute taking skills were also exceptional, as was her Dictaphone technique, making her a prime candidate for the position of personal assistant in any government department. What Sarah had not realised at the time of the eleventh-hour request was that her commitment to duty was being tested. A test she was expected to pass with flying colours.

*****

"How is it going, Josie?" Stan, the porter, asked, popping his head around one of the double doors.

"Not too bad. At a bit of a standstill, if I'm honest, but all present and correct at the moment," Josie said. "The fog isn't lifting much though, but fingers crossed it will start to soon and everything will get sorted. I think at least one of them will be on their way home soon," she said, nodding towards the little group.

45

"Did you hear that?" Fred, said. "One of us will be getting out of here soon! Eureka! Now who, I wonder will lady-luck smile on first?"

"It will definitely be me. My Edward must be on his way to me," Penelope, said.

Clarissa looked into the eyes of her baby son and whispered, "it won't be long now. We will be going home soon."

"Does anyone know what time the next train to London, Euston is due?" Sarah asked.

CHAPTER
SEVEN

Fred, despite his mother's reasoning and plea-bargaining, was standing to attention on the front line of the passing-out parade having successfully completed an intensive training course, which, needless to say, he passed with flying colours. In fact, he was awarded the accolade, 'Best New Recruit'. His friend Billy, equally as proud, stood as straight as a dye, on the righthand side of him. The Royal Artillery was their chosen regiment although, at the time, neither of them had really grasped what belonging to such a prestigious regiment entailed. All too soon, they would discover the truth and depth of the status. His mother had tried, in vain, to warn him of the dangers he may face, but there is none so deaf as those who refuse to heed wise advice, especially from their elders.

Before being posted, Fred and Billy, his faithful sidekick, underwent sixteen weeks of basic training. Stepping through the gates to the facility they felt euphoric. A new start in accommodation which, for all the world, reminded them of a prison, although neither of them voiced any trepidation. Induction, after roll call, started immediately. Fred, overflowing with bravado, was first in line to have his head shaved and had no objection to the shearing but Billy, who had a healthy crop of jet-black, thick hair, instantly felt naked, bereft and more than a tad humiliated. Having lost his most attractive feature, he felt cold and habitually rubbed his hands over the stumpy bristles. Sadly, the loss of his attractive mane would prove insignificant in the light of his destiny. Fitness training, weapon handling and using live ammunition were the order of the day. What faced them on deployments would be a test of sheer brute force and determination, coupled with honour, service and duty. The thoroughness of training and discipline was paramount. Perhaps it was not quite what they had both expected army life to be like but, in Fred's book, it beat working on the coalface by a mile. In his letters to his mother, he told her that he had taken to the army like a duck takes to water, one of her pet phrases. Billy, for his part, trusted Fred's judgement and believed they were in the best place in the world. Then again, he would have followed Fred anywhere and everywhere. He owed him so much and this spat was just another hurdle, and not a very high one, on their mutual road to freedom and a better life.

"If we do as we are told, we will both do well, Billy," Fred, said. "Think of it as a learning curve. Besides, what have we got to lose? There's nothing for us in civvy street apart from dead-end jobs. This will set us up for life. All manner of professions will be queuing up with job offers when we're discharged but we'll turn them all down an' become partners. It doesn't really matter what we are partners in as long as it's not partners in crime, hey?" he joked.

"Well, if you fell into a bucketful of muck, head first, you would come up smelling of roses. Therefore, in Fred and Partners, I will trust," Billy said, standing to attention and saluting his friend.

"You stick with me Billy and we'll get through whatever they throw at us together. Tomorrow is a new day," Fred said. "So, make sure to get your arse in gear, it's overdrive we both need to be in. All we have got to do is keep our heads down, and our gunpowder dry. At least I think that's the trick and, I have it on good authority, that it is a tried and tested one."

Billy didn't respond or flinch. His feet, in fact his entire body, had started to feel cold.

*****

"Where are we going, poppa?" Penelope asked, dragging her feet along the heavily patterned, hall carpet.

"This way," he said, making for the staircase and the galleried landing. "Are you keeping up with us, nanny?"

"Yes, sir," she gasped.

"Why are we going upstairs? My Champion will not be up here. He must be in the stables." Her father stopped and stooped down. As gently as he could, he said: "there is no Champion, Penelope. Your pony will have to wait a little longer, but I do have a wonderful surprise for you. This way."

Penelope's chin was almost resting on her tiny chest when she was literally dragged into her parents' boudoir. There, pillowed-up in the middle of an antique, four-poster bed, was her step-mother, dressed in a luxurious, French silk, nightgown and pale-blue, bed jacket. Her jet black, curly hair gently brushed her shoulders.

49

"Do come and sit by me, Penelope," her step-mother, said, patting a spot, on top of the bed. "We have brought you something very special back from London. Something that no amount of money can buy. Penelope this is Sophie, your new baby sister. Isn't she beautiful?"

"A baby! A sister! I don't want that! I do not want her; I do **not** want a sister. Take her back, poppa, please take her back to London. I want a pony. You promised me that I would have my own horse. I do not want her," she cried, screaming and stamping her feet by the side of the bed to the shock of everyone present, apart from nanny.

"That's enough, Penelope," her father, said. "I am confident that you and Sophie will become the very best of friends."

"We will never be friends. I wanted a pony, poppa. Not a sister."

"I know, princess, and I promise you that your steed will be in our stables soon. Now, be a good girl and dry those tears. Nanny, would you kindly escort Miss Penelope to the nursery, please? I will speak with her again, later. The poor girl is in a state of shock. One thought you may have prepared her for this. Obviously not." Nanny dutifully obeyed.

Penelope's step-mother sank back into the huge pillows, supporting her back. The pregnancy had been unplanned and unexpected and the delivery of her daughter had completely exhausted her. Complications during her final trimester confined her to one of the finest hospitals in London, without whose expertise she may not only have lost the baby but her own life, as well. Penelope had been spared the details of the pregnancy and birth, fearing that her step-sister, at the very least, would be lost. As it was, mother and child both survived the ordeal and were thriving. Life would never be the same for Penelope and, at almost ten years of age, she hated and resented the thought of change, whatever it brought. She hated Sophie almost as fiercely as she hated her step-mother who would never come close to replacing her very own mummy, who had tragically died of influenza, on Penelope's fifth birthday.

*****

Clarissa had lost every ounce of interest in her studies and easily relinquished her dreams of university. No longer passionate about examination results, entry requirements and qualifications, her future, she was sure, lay with Darren, her first love. As a consequence, she spent less and less time studying and missed lots of important lectures. Her grades plummeted, leaving her mother distraught. She could read Clarissa like a book and was determined to do everything in her power to challenge her waywardness.

"Please don't throw your life away on someone you have only just met, Clarissa. Who is he, anyway? At least tell me his name. Your father and I would like to meet him."

"Meet him! What for? Meet him so that you can tell him where to get off to. You have got no chance of meeting him because I know, without doubt, you would object to him as soon as you laid eyes on him. You, who judge a book purely by its cover, would reject him and because of that you will never meet him."

"But, you are throwing your opportunities to the wind and I am asking you, begging you, not to do it. Qualifications last a lifetime. Please think logically about it. No man is worth it, especially one that you have only just met."

"Wrong again, mother, dear. There are more important things in life than bits of paper with exam results and degree grades written on them. Afterall, is that what truly defines us? Bits of paper based on an examiner's assessment of our worth - or lack of it! We are all more than that. Flesh and blood; emotions and feelings; the fulfilment of hopes and dreams, are they not worthy ambitions, too? To know, without doubt, that we are loved and totally accepted by someone else. How much is that worth in your estimation of life, mother?"

"There is no reasoning with you, Clarissa. We have loved you with an unconditional love since the day you were born. But, it is indeed your life and you will live with the consequences of your choices, along with the rest of us. We can only a lead a horse to water, we cannot make it drink! But, mark my words and mark them well, somewhere along the line, you may regret missed opportunities."

"Here we go again. And, who, I wonder is on their high horse now?"

The room sighed, heavy with the weight of resignation. No parent, with the best will in the world, can live their child's life for them, including those who only have their best interests at heart. No one can choose a pathway for another however much they are loved. The gift of freedom,

freedom to choose, to err, to learn from one's mistakes, may prove, given time, to be a worthwhile education. Yet, surely any parent, would save their child the anguish of remorse and regret if they possibly could. Even birds guard and defend the nests of their young, protecting them from predators.

*****

Sarah along with every other stenographer in the typing pool never stopped to take a break. Time was of the essence and the continual battering of typewriter keys and carriages returning, was deafening. Her own desktop was always orderly. A black Remington typewriter sat in pride of place, central to everything, including a shorthand notebook and pencil, the latest Dictaphone transcription machine, a ream of letterheaded paper, a box of carbon paper, alongside a perfectly positioned typewriter rubber, not that Sarah succumbed to using it very often. Every piece of her work was print-perfect.

"Can you spare a moment, Miss Worth, please?" the government's top official, asked.

Sarah immediately thought that she had made an error in one of her transcripts, a vitally important one. She had recently transcribed a record of an important inquiry and although she had double-checked her work, she doubted her own ability. Underneath her air of confidence, lived a 'Doubting Thomas'.

"Please, take a seat," he said, before sitting down himself. "I will cut to the chase, my dear. I have good news for you. Life-changing news, in fact. You have been selected for an extremely important, confidential and delicate task within government's central office. Accuracy, reliability and competence are paramount and you, Miss Worth, are the best we have and perfectly fit the bill. I have been asked to endorse a temporary contract for you," he said, passing a large, brown envelope across the highly-polished, desk. "Please let me have your decision by noon tomorrow, at the latest. I would emphasise that this is a career opportunity not to be missed and one which, I have little doubt, you will grasp with both hands. There is, I hasten to add, a permanent position in the pipeline, with your name on it, following the successful completion of the assignment contained within this document," he said, nudging the envelope towards her with the end of his pipe.

"Thank you, sir. I feel... honoured. A little shocked perhaps, but honoured, nonetheless."

The official smirked. "Do not let it go to your head, my dear. There is long line of ladies, sitting behind typewriters out there, who would put up a fight for this position. You have been singled out because you are conscientious and committed. In a nutshell, your dedication and high standards have been noted and are being generously rewarded."

It was not the time to ask questions. Sarah stood up to leave, feeling rather like a jellified dessert being served on a silver platter.

"Thank you, sir," she repeated.

"I look forward to receiving your acceptance of the contract by noon tomorrow, Miss Worth. Having highly recommended you for the position I am confident that you will not let me down."

"I am quite sure that the contract will be more than acceptable to me, sir, and, I have no doubt that you will receive my agreement by noon tomorrow," she said, regaining some of her composure before turning to leave.

"That is awfully reassuring. I am confident that you will pull out all the stops and make an excellent job of the offer. It will be an outstanding reflection, ultimate recognition of the standards we uphold and maintain in this neck of the woods. I do hope London will value your contribution as much as we have. Raise your sights. The Prime Minister is keen to employ stenographers of your calibre and the corridors of Westminster are yours for the taking. Congratulations, Miss Worth. Make sure to do us proud."

"London. Did he just say London?" she muttered, under her breath, returning to the typing pool.

*****

Fred completed another circle of the waiting room and glanced at the wall clock, again.

"Don't get too excited comrades, but I think the fog is starting to lift, a bit. I'm sure it is not quite as dense out there," he said.

His three counterparts joined him at the window.

"I do think, on this occasion, you may be right, Frederick," Penelope said.

"Well, that's a first, Madame Smithson. I never thought you would agree with me about anything!"

Penelope ignored him.

"I am sure someone will be here for us soon," Clarissa whispered to her baby. "And, I think we will definitely call you Archie, after your grandfather. We'll be home soon."

"Well, I am packed and ready to leave," Sarah said, slumping back into a chair. "Just need my ticket to London, Euston and I'll be off."

Fred, however, was frozen in time.

CHAPTER EIGHT

"Let's doublecheck everything is spick and span before inspection, Billy. No slacking, we don't want to be caught out. We've got everything in the bag, even if it is a kit bag!" Fred, joked. "And, I've heard on the grapevine, as the best new recruit by a mile, that we will be getting a posting soon. Our first round of duty is just around the corner."

Billy, with both hands behind his head, was lying on top of the narrow, army bed in the billet. "Wonder where we'll be sent?" he said, gazing at the ceiling.

"Could be the other side of the world for all I care. The sky's the limit for us, Billy."

"To be honest, Fred, I don't know if I'm up for it. If the army life is for me, I mean."

"What on earth are you talking about, Billy? Of course, it's for you. What else are you going to do, deliver newspapers all your life? I have no idea where we'll be posted but I promised you that we would see the world, and we will. Wherever we end up it will be a million times better than being sent down the belly of a mine. Coal dust in every pore, suffocating our lungs. Stick with me and I promise that you will be fine. You know I've got your back, always have and always will. Now stop moping around and let's get on with checking our uniforms. We need to make sure our kit is one hundred percent ready. Socks, pants, jumper, shirts, tie, and vests. I can definitely see the reflection of my handsome mug in these boots. Better than any mirror they are."

"I'm not checking anything again, Fred. If we don't pass inspection no one will. And, to be honest, none of this is what I expected it to be." Fred didn't have time to reassure Billy, his right-hand man, that everything would be hunky-dory. The door to the billet burst open. It was September 3, 1939.

"Prime Minister, Neville Chamberlain, has declared war on Germany after their invasion of Poland," Pete, another recruit, called. "We'll be in the thick of it soon, so best foot forward lads!"

"Did you hear that, Billy? We are at war and will, no doubt, be touring Europe soon."

"There's something else, lads," Pete, the news-bearer, said. "I've heard, from a good source, that we are on a warning for duty in a war-torn, secret location." The billet fell silent. No one moved a muscle in response to Pete's whispered revelation.

Childhood games of cowboys and Indians, knights of the round table, Ivanhoe and Robin Hood were, without doubt, dead and buried. Memories of wooden swords, bows and arrows, not to mention the faithful camaraderie of Silver and Samson, his fleet of two, were quickly replaced by the reality of huge guns, mounted on artillery vehicles and the loading and unloading of weapons with live ammunition. 'Magazine off, cock, hook and look,' became their united mantra and rumbled around their heads, day and night, causing twitches and tics in every part of their bodies. Only the strongest survived the most intensive training and drills. Throughout it all, one childhood truth remained stable, immoveable, amid the fearful commotion. Fred and Billy were bound together. Whatever the future held they had each other's back.

*****

"Come along now, Penelope, crying over spilt milk never did anyone any good," nanny, said. "Besides, you are very lucky to have a beautiful baby sister not to mention a mother and father who love you dearly. You have so much to thank God, for my dear."

"I am only thankful to God for giving me those things which I want, nanny, and I want a pony of my own. I do not want a step-sister and she is not beautiful. I am beautiful. And her mother is not my mummy. My mummy is dead," she spat.

The passing of time and events did not change Penelope's feelings or attitude. In fact, the increasing intensity of them became unnerving, unsettling.

Standing over Sophie's crib in the nursery, Penelope was obediently rocking her three-month old sister to sleep. Nanny hoped that being close to Sophie would aid Penelope's acceptance and love of her. Just as Sophie was closing her eyes, Penelope bent over to kiss her on her cheek and whispered: "I wish you had never been born. I hate you. I will always hate you".

59

"Well done, Miss Penelope. Baby Sophie is fast asleep. What a kind, big sister you are," nanny, said.

Penelope put her hand over her mouth and sniggered. She had fooled everyone in the dangerous game she was playing and was determined, as ever, to win.

*****

Sarah's feet barely touched the floor on her way home from the government office. This was the chance she had been waiting for, the chance of a lifetime. An open door in the corridors of power marked 'Opportunity and Freedom'.

As she climbed the stairs, leading to the insalubrious, tenement block her excitement started to evaporate and was slowly replaced by reason and reality. Fact overtook fancy. Perhaps there would be no escape from the filth of where she lived, who she really was, underneath the respectable clothes she wore to the office. In her position as top stenographer, she could at least pretend that she belonged, that she was a woman of worth, of some value even, but with every step she climbed, the shouts of abuse raging behind the doors she passed, underlined the truth of the matter. She turned the key in the lock to her home, her hovel. The room was dark and damp, but scrubbed clean.

"How are you mother? Have you had a good day?" she called, as she entered the room.

"I'm fine, precious. Just fine," her mother said. "Never mind me, how has your day been?"

"As good as days go, mom. I was offered…, offered…"

"Offered what? What were you offered, Sarah?"

"A cup of tea. I was offered a cup of tea, mom, that's all. Talking of which, I'll put the stove on. I've picked up a treat for us from the deli on the corner," she said, walking towards an old, gas stove in the dimly-lit, kitchen area.

Sarah grasped the top of the blue stove with both hands. Her head bent, her heart about to break with the weight of reality. She would never leave her mother. Never escape the tenement block. How could she possibly move to London to selfishly seek the fulfilment of her own dreams, ambitions and prospects? Who would care for her mother, especially if her health continued to deteriorate? Sarah's life, too, was ebbing away, dissipating through her fingertips. Reluctantly, she slowly acknowledged that there would be no escape from the stench and squalor, for Sarah Worth. This was the reality of the situation and this was where her sort belonged and no number of contracts, well-deserved or not, would change that fact.

Slowly she took off her smart, top-stenographer clothes and neatly folded them up, placing them on a shelf in an old cupboard. She positioned the brown envelope, containing her hopes of a new life, on top of them before closing the door.

CHAPTER NINE

The telephone rang, almost continually, in the discharge lounge. Josie switched it to answer machine enabling her to wade through some outstanding paperwork. There was far too much red tape in this important hospital department for her liking.

"All shipshape?" Stan, asked, striding towards the reception desk.

"As good as it can be, given the conditions and circumstances," Josie said, looking past the patients into the swirling fog, outside.

"They are not all still here, are they?" he said. "I thought you would have at least sent one of them packing by now!" he whispered, leaning over the reception desk.

"There is not much I can do about it, is there? Look at it. You can't see a hand in front of your face out there. Apparently, traffic is at a standstill and, I can barely believe my ears, Stanley. Did you just say, 'sent one of them packing'? May I remind you that we are duty bound to provide a respectful, supportive service, regardless of the hurdles we may encounter," she said.

"Sorry, it was just a slip of the tongue. I didn't mean to offend. The service is pressurised on the best of days and the weather conditions often add to the stress. Hopefully, it won't delay our plans for later though. I think we both need some downtime," Stan, boldly said.

"I am sure it won't and, if need be, I will hand over to the next shift, but hopefully everyone will have been discharged by six. I cannot control the impact of the weather conditions on our service, though, can I? I'm not Houdini! What time did you say you finish?"

"Five, if there is nothing last minute. I'll just have time to recharge my batteries before our date. You don't mind if I call it a date, do you?" Josie's smile gave away her answer. They had tiptoed around their feelings for each other for months and risked losing their once-in-a-lifetime chance of love.

"Well, if I don't get chance to pop in again, I will call back for you at six, if that's ok?"

"That's fine. I can almost taste a G&T," she said, as Stan disappeared through the door.

"Well, that says it all, doesn't it?" Fred said, turning to face the three other detainees. "They can't wait to go to the bleedin' pub! So much for all that devotion crap!"

"I would be most grateful if you would refrain from using that type of language," Penelope said. "Besides, we have a child in our midst."

"Don't be so bleedin' daft Madame Smithson! Baby Archie will not be able to remember anything about today, will he, Clarissa?"

"Please do not include me or my little one in your disagreements," Clarissa, said.

"What's your take on it, Sarah? You have no objections to a bit of tasteful banter, have you?"

"I have heard worse, Fred. Delays can be frustrating and life's irritations generally bring out the worst in all of us. Let's try to remain understanding and respectful. It's the least we can do. Anyway, why don't you sit down, Fred? You have been staring into that fog for far too long."

"Well said, Sarah," Penelope, said.

"Well said!" Fred, piped up. "Well, bleedin' said! You will be suggesting that we all play 'I spy with my little eye' next!"

"It may be nice to get to know each other a bit more. Besides, it would pass the time and we may discover that we have more in common than we think," Clarissa said.

"I, for one, would not partake in any self-indulgent, party games. What could I possibly have in common with any of you?" Penelope said, unbuttoning the top button of her pure wool coat, again, whilst moving to sit on the opposite side of the room.

"Since it was your suggestion, Clarissa, perhaps you would like to start us off by telling us a bit more about yourself. I think they call it sharing, these days," Sarah, said.

"Yes, you can start the bleedin' ball rolling, Miss Clarissa," It is 'Miss' isn't it?" Fred, said.

Clarissa looked down at her baby's, tiny face. "It is Miss and I am not ashamed of that. I thought I would be, but I am not. I was seventeen when I met Darren, my son's father…"

*****

"You aren't going out again, are you, Clarissa?" her mother, asked. "Why don't you get some revision done? Your exams will be on top of you before you know it, so don't leave revising until the last minute. Cramming doesn't work!"

"What would you know about cramming or anything else to do with exams, mum? What qualifications have you got? None at the last count!"

"That's true, but I was denied the opportunities you've had served to you on a plate, young lady! Kindly remember that fact the next time you are reckoning up my qualifications, or lack of them!"

"Not that old chestnut, again. Why don't you give it a rest mum? Everyone and their dog as heard that you were denied an education, but there are more important things in life. And, by the way, I *will* be going out again tonight and you can't stop me, so don't even try."

Violet resigned herself to the situation and busied herself with household duties. Perhaps she was trying to live some of her missed opportunities, through her daughter's life. But, then again, she only wanted the very best for her and, in her book, education was an integral feature of success. On the other hand, it could be argued, that without gaining a single qualification, some chancers succeed, although numerically, such were few and far between. Fortune and fame usually went hand-in-hand with hard work and qualifications were generally the preferred, if not essential, passport into ever career, enhancing the holder's prospects in the process. Therefore, why wouldn't a mother want the best education possible for their child?

"I've made it, Darren," Clarissa, said. "Not without a struggle, though. Mum isn't a happy bunny. She thinks I should be studying. Mind you, I have got my 'A' levels in a few weeks but they don't seem important to me now," she said, shrugging her shoulders.

"I don't want to be a stumbling block in your life, Clarissa. Just because I bunked off school and am doing well enough, doesn't mean that everyone who opts for the less conventional route will."

"I have told mum, in no uncertain terms, that there are more important things in life than exams but she's only got a one-track mind! Education, education and yes, you've guessed it, Darren, more education!"

"Sounds like she only wants the best for you, though. My mother didn't care where I was or what I was up to. Everything boiled down to the luck-of-the-draw and I'm only on track now because someone believed in me and gave me a chance, a leg-up. I will still work hard, though, especially for you. Then again, I have got more to prove than most, haven't I? Wonder what your mother would make of me? Do you think your parents would like me? Approve of us, I mean?"

Clarissa was stumped. Should she tell him the truth, spill the beans and risk losing him, or leave him guessing, hopeful of acceptance?

"Dad wouldn't let you put a foot over our front door, Darren. Mum may be more tolerant, but dad would only see the colour of your skin. He doesn't believe in mixed relationships, says they come with too much baggage, too many hurdles and, in his book, life has its fair share of those without adding to them."

The round, brass-topped, table for two in the corner of The Swan fell silent as the realisation of the cost of their young love momentarily overwhelmed them.

"So much for not judging a book by its cover then?" Darren, eventually said, turning his pint pot round.

"Prejudice, in any shape, form or opinion, is distorted and ugly. Together, our love will challenge it, overcome it and destroy its power," she said, taking his hand in her own. "We will look prejudice straight in the eye and demand it concedes to our love."

"I wish it was that easy, Claris. I have been looking into the eyes of prejudice, head on, every day of my life, and little has changed. In fact, I have never seen it blink, not once. Do you know what happened, a short time ago, to Doctor Martin Luther King, Junior? Well do you?

I think I've heard his name. Was he killed, murdered?

"He was one of the most prominent people in the civil rights movement in the United States of America, a voice for the persecuted, until the day he was assassinated and silenced in 1968. Shot him dead, they did. He had a dream, Clarissa, a dream of freedom and equality for all people, a civil rights dream which would end racism. He was a brave, bold man whose dreams and inspirational words condemned him to death. It seems so futile now, because, years later, I am still being mocked and persecuted for the colour of my skin. Your love for me will, in many ways, cost you your life and I will not let you pay that price. Your mother and father are right, there are too many hurdles on our track."

"But they didn't silence him, did they? I know about the speech you are talking about and its words and precepts are more alive and pertinent today than when he delivered them. He was not silenced. He will never be silenced. If anything, his death poured fuel on freedom's fire and whatever it costs me, I will love you. I will stare into the eyes of prejudice alongside you and together our love, our union, will beat it into the ground," she said, relinquishing her dreams of university and laying them at his feet.

CHAPTER TEN

"You've gone very quiet, Sarah. Cat got your tongue?" Fred, asked.

"I have also had my share of hurdles on my path through life," Sarah said, turning to face Clarissa. "Life can be so cruel, unjust and unfair. It is certainly not all plain sailing, is it? I chose to relinquish my own ambitions many years ago…"

*****

"Could I see you, sir?" Sarah asked the government official, picking up the brown envelope containing the contract of employment.

"Of course, Miss Worth. Do come through. Take a seat. Thank you for signing and returning your contract. I have already spoken to Westminster. They are eager to meet you and are busy preparing for your arrival. In fact, they cannot wait for you to join their team. I have taken the liberty of booking you a ticket on the London, Euston train on Monday next, an indication of the urgency and sensitivity of the job in hand. The sooner you get down there the better it will be for everyone concerned. I cannot begin to tell you how delighted I am that one of my 'girls' will be filling such an important role in Westminster. It is undoubtedly a feather in both of our caps," he said, refilling his pipe with tobacco.

"About the contract, sir," she said, placing the large, brown envelope in the middle of his oversized, solid wood desk. "I will not be able to accept the terms of the contract. Unfortunately…"

"Stop, right there, Miss Worth! What on earth is the meaning of this? You cannot possibly be serious. No one refuses a position in Westminster, especially one I have personally recommended and endorsed them for. Now kindly reconsider, immediately," he said, forcefully sliding the contract back towards her.

"I am unable to reconsider, sir. I have personal obligations which have overruled my ability to accept the position. I am unable to sign the contract.

"Personal obligations! What are you talking about? You do not have a child, children, do you? We do not usually employ women of childbearing age, but as you are unmarried, we assumed that you did not have any personal obligations, particularly in the form of a child or children! Would you care to enlighten me, Miss Worth?"

"I would not care to do so, sir. In fact, I will not enlighten you further. It is with regret that I must decline the offer of promotion and a train ticket to London, Euston."

"Then you, Miss Worth, are dismissed. Kindly ask Miss Wentworth, who will, no doubt, be delighted to fill your shoes, to join me on your way out."

"Dismissed, sir?"

"That is correct. You are dismissed. Take your personal belongings with you when you vacate the premises. Your services are no longer required in this government office. No one is irreplaceable and that includes you, Miss Worthless."

Sarah never mentioned the position in London, her decision to decline the offer and her heartbreak at having done so, to her mother. There was little point. All too quickly, her mother appeared to be disappearing into her own world and there was little that Sarah, or anyone else, could do to prevent or slow its progression. As a child, Sarah had watched her grandmother slowly disappear, devoured by forgetfulness, until one day, one dreadful day, she no longer recognised those whom she had loved for a lifetime. Dementia's cruel, bottomless abyss knew no mercy and her grandmother plummeted into its oblivion, a place where she no longer recognised her own daughter. For her part, Sarah watched from the sidelines as her mother lovingly cared for her grandmother whom she promised never to leave nor forsake, regardless of whether her mother remembered her, or not. Such devotion found a resting place in Sarah's young heart and she determined, if necessary, to be as kind to her own mother as her mother had been to her grandmother. Senile diseases are ruthless and no respecter of persons, position or affluence. Sarah recognised the early signs of the disease and feared that her own mother was teetering on the edge of it, staring into its black, bottomless, pit. She would not abandon her for a ticket to the moon, let alone one to London, Euston.

Having been dismissed from her permanent position Sarah grasped whatever temporary positions, via an agency, became available and which she could manage, more easily, around her commitments. Every penny of her government severance pay disappeared on the services of a day-care agency which enabled her to work and provide a roof, albeit a modest one, over their heads and put food onto their table.

Sarah was working as a temporary cashier, covering maternity leave, in a local bank, when the tide of her life began to turn in her favour. Her ability and attention to detail had not gone unnoticed and, towards the end of her tenure, the bank manager invited her to join him for a business lunch. Wearing her stenographer's suit which, if nothing else, concealed her true identity, she quickly cleaned and polished her shoes in the ladies' power room, believing that shoes were the most tell-tale items of clothing.

The luncheon took place in a local, high-class hotel. Sarah, although initially uncomfortable, did not look a tad out of place. On the contrary, she looked every bit the part. A smart, professional woman, oozing confidence. Mr Davies, the manager, held out a chair at the table for her to sit down. His manners were impeccable, although there was nothing intriguing or attractive about his opaque appearance and bland persona. Members of staff, at the bank, labelled him, 'Mr Boring Average Man', when he was not within earshot of their quips, of course. The small, round table donning a white, starched cloth, was perfectly laid. The lunch menu was varied and upper crust.

"Would you prefer white or red with your appetiser?" the waiter, dressed in a penguin-suit, asked, whilst standing to attention, poised to take their order." Sarah almost turned to him to ask what he would recommend, but decided against it. She needed to demonstrate that she had a mind, a strong mind, of her own. She was more than a cashier, come stenographer, at least at lunchtime, in a salubrious restaurant.

"Just water, please," she said, holding her hand over the top of the wine glass. "I do not usually partake of alcoholic beverages during the day and certainly not at business meetings."

"Red, for me, Beaujolais," Mr Davies, said. The waiter, with one arm behind his back and a white cloth, draped over the other, dutifully poured the wine, placing the bottle onto the table. "Now then, please tell me more about yourself, Miss Worth, kindly indulge me. I notice you worked for the government, as a stenographer. Why did you resign from that position? You did resign, didn't you?"

"Yes, I held a government position, and felt very fortunate and proud to do so. My resignation from office was more by mutual agreement, sir."

"Please, call me William, at least in this setting."

"I was selected to fill an important position in Westminster, a once-in-a-lifetime opportunity and one which I would have relished, had I not been forced to decline. After the event, I decided to move on, spread my net and stretch my wings in order to broaden my experience and expertise.

"Would it be impertinent to ask why you turned the offer down? It would have been an amazing stepping stone and would, no doubt, have been financially rewarding. Do you have children, a family?

"No. I am not an unmarried mother, nothing like that. I do have family commitments to consider, though. I live with my mother who needs... my support." Mr Davies, sighed.

"I am not aware of any other young lady, especially one of your calibre and character, who would sacrifice such an opportunity in the interests of a parent's welfare," he said, raising his wine glass to his lips. Sarah straightened her back.

"Surely duty should be an important feature in everyone's life and perhaps even a deciding factor in our options and choices. It is my opinion, William, that we must all live with the consequences of the decisions we make in the light of our responsibilities to those we love. That is the very least we owe them," she said, smoothing down the pure white, table cloth.

"Miss Worth, Sarah," William said, leaning slightly towards her. "I have no hesitation in offering you another temporary position with us. In truth, I am delighted to offer you the post. We can discuss the terms of your flexible contract and salary back at the office. They will be terms, which I hope will allow you to continue to support your mother and ones that we will regularly review together."

"Thank you, William. I am sure the terms will be acceptable and I am grateful to you for the offer and the opportunity you have afforded me. I will not let you down."

"Good! Very good! Now, let us enjoy our first of many business lunches together. It looks delicious, doesn't it?" Sarah smiled.

CHAPTER
ELEVEN

"It would be interesting to hear about your very *privileged* life, Madame Smithson," Fred said, joining her on the opposite side of the room. "Bet you haven't half got some tales you could tell us. Spice up the time a bit," he said, glancing at the clock.

"I have little doubt that my experiences will have been far more refined and immensely more sedate, than your own, Frederick. On the other hand, one appreciates that your life, your story, will have been far more colourful than my own and certainly more entertaining. Perhaps your recollections may even make time itself standstill for us."

"I'll give you that much, Madame, and I must admit that my life has, without doubt, been far more colourful, more vivid, than your own. I get the impression, the feeling, that yours has been rather elitist, I think that's what they call something snobby these days. Mine was anything but..."

****

To Fred's disappointment, no one was waiting to fling their arms around them, when, with Billy in tow, they stepped off a plane onto European soil. Neither of the young men had flown anywhere before and both felt a bit queasy from the experience, although Fred refused to admit or show any sign of it. Prior to the flight, the furthest from home the two had travelled was to Rhyl, a seaside town in north Wales, not counting their passing out parade, of course.

Despite his bravado and excitement, Fred felt uneasy, anxious about Billy. Had he let his friend down, misled him and sold him a life of adventure, which may well turn sour at the drop of a hat? Then again, it was early days, and his mother had regularly reminded him that 'everything, given time, comes out in the wash'. He hoped the saying was true, because his father had also told him, the last time he had seen him, that, if nothing else, the army would make a man out of him. Perhaps he should have known better than to believe and trust in anything his father, who had deserted them, told him. Yet, he chose to believe that everything would go to plan and a pot of gold would indeed be waiting for them at the end of their army service rainbow, war or not. He just needed to help Billy to find his feet and establish his future in the forces alongside him.

"I'm sure we'll get some downtime, Billy. I promise you it won't be all work and no play, even if we are at war, and when we do get time off we won't half paint the nearest town red. I have it on good authority that they will welcome us with open arms here and it wouldn't surprise me if they rolled out the red carpet for us two." Billy didn't reply, he threw his kit bag over his shoulder and continued walking. His thoughts were miles away. He was a home bird at heart and was yearning for his familiar, secure nest.

The only thing awaiting the band of brothers at their destination was emergency training, and lots of it. Physical fitness was paramount and at the top of the agenda, followed by weapon handling and target practice. The firing ranges, especially without headgear, were deafening. Written, verbal and non-verbal communication skills were also the order of the day, coupled with navigation and intelligence training. Every skill, and there was too many to number, needed to be finely and quickly honed, they had to be because lives depended on them and comrades depended on each other.

It was at the end of a particularly gruelling day, after downing a few beers, that Fred's concerns, his sixth sense, about Billy were confirmed.

"Could you shoot someone and kill them, Fred?" Billy asked. "We are not playing cowboys and Indians now, are we? This is for real and rumour is we will be in the thick of live combat soon. Could you blow someone's head off? Well, could you, Fred?"

"Well, it's dog eat dog, isn't it? If we don't shoot them, they will shoot us. We've not signed up for a Sunday-school tea-party, have we? Life could always be worse. What about Bevin's boys, young men, like us, who are being chosen by lot to work as miners. They have no choice or say in the matter and are being forced to work down the pit, what's more, I bet they won't receive any recognition for coughing their lungs up. Look, we are here to serve our King and country and we've enrolled to do our duty and, by God's grace, that is exactly what we will do."

"Since when has it been our duty to kill people, Fred?"

"Look, Billy, it goes with the territory, with the job."

"That's what I thought you would say. But what if I can't do it, Fred? What if I can't shoot someone dead? What if I can't be like you, like you want me to be? I've read about soldiers who were on the front-line during the first world war who couldn't hack it. And, you know what happened to them, don't you? They were court marshalled and led out at dawn, shaking from shellshock, to be shot as cowards by their own battalions. Could you do that, Fred? Shoot one of our own, because he had lost his nerve, probably suffering from post-traumatic stress. Well, could you? Could you shoot me?"

"Life is not perfect, Billy. The services aren't perfect. Nothing is, and no one is always right about everything. But, we have signed up, enlisted, and by God we will do our duty for our King and country and we will cross the bridges on our path when we get to them and not before. We are in this together and I'll tell you this much, if someone was going to shoot you, blow *your* head off, I would kill them in a heartbeat. Don't be kidding yourself about the enemy. We are not bleedin' missionaries; we are learning how to protect and defend everything dear to us and we will give death a run for its money if it dares to come knocking on our door. Mind you, it would have to be quick to catch us, especially if we move as fast as we did on Silver and Sampson."

"Ok, lone ranger, you can climb down off your high horse. I have to agree with you and do appreciate where you are coming from. To be honest, I'm proud to wear my uniform and represent the country of my birth. It's just that I'm not sure what's right and wrong anymore. I even carry my father's army bible in my kitbag with me. Apparently, the bible was a core part of a soldier's kit and, according to my dad, a source of hope in times of desperation and despair. He was issued with it when he served in the war that was supposed to end all wars and he gave it to me on the day I enlisted. He made me promise him that I would keep it close to me, and I will. Fancy being issued with a bible when he was being sent to fight in a war. Don't get me wrong, it's not that I've read it from cover to cover, but it's comforting to know that my dad had faith in its words and lived to tell the tale. But, then again, nothing is ever all black or all white, is it? One thing is crystal clear, we will be in the thick of it soon enough."

"Well, if you don't know the difference between good and evil now, you never will, and heaven help us. There are two forces at work in this world, Billy, and I know whose side I want to be counted on. What's more, I will face whoever or whatever I have to, head on. There'll be no bullet holes in my back. Now get some shut-eye. We've got another big day ahead of us tomorrow."

Billy turned over and opened his Father's bible. "The Lord is my shepherd, I shall not want," he whispered into the darkness.

*****

"You haven't fallen asleep again, have you Madame Smithson?" Frederick asked. "Surely your son can't be much longer, especially if he's driving a roller! His privileged starting blocks must have given him a massive head start in life; miles ahead of us commoners on the circuit track," Fred said, pulling up a chair alongside her. "Look, class distinction aside, can I get you a brew? Think you could do with one. Perk you up a bit. You've turned terribly pale."

80

"That is awfully considerate of you, Frederick, but I am not one to drink from cardboard cups. I have sipped my tea from the best porcelain in the world, Royal Doulton no less, from a very early age," she said, placing her head on the backrest and closing her eyes, oblivious to what she was about to see.

*****

"I am so excited about Sophie's birthday party, Miss Penelope," nanny said. "I do hope the sun shines on us. We are planning a big celebration on the front lawn and, I understand, some of your friends may join us."

"Have you been daydreaming again, nanny or just indulging in another game of Happy Families? You cannot possibly believe that any of my friends possess the slightest interest in, or desire to attend, my step-sister's birthday soiree. Indeed, it is highly unlikely that I will be in attendance. I will be awfully busy on that day."

"Oh! Miss Penelope, you must attend, she is your sister and she will be so disappointed if you do not feature in her celebrations."

"I do not have to do anything I do not wish to do, nanny and she is not my sister, far from it. Besides, I will be a teenager soon and that is the only thing I am truly excited about. A third birthday party is rather unpalatable, boring. No doubt, you will be busy baking her a cake?" she said, before yawning.

"I definitely will. A beautiful pink cake, with ribbons and bows fit for a princess. She looks every inch a princess, doesn't she? I have had a sneak preview of her party dress.

It has come all the way from France. I have never seen anything quite like it in all my years. Have you?"

"Why on earth would I want to look at a three-year old's party dress? If you must know, I simply cannot abide someone else's fuss and nonsense, nanny. I have nothing in common with Sophie. In truth, I find her rather dull and extremely childish. She cramps my style. Anyway, when can we get down to planning *my* thirteenth birthday? Poppa has told me that I can have a marque on the lawn. A huge marque, with a circus, my very own circus. Now *that* is something to get excited about, isn't it? Everyone, but everyone who is anyone, will be begging to be invited. It will be the event of the year and will certainly overshadow Sophie's little soiree, not that I would intentionally want to do that, you understand. It is simply a foregone conclusion, though."

"Will you excuse me, Miss Penelope? I need to prepare your father's tea-tray," nanny, said.

"Very well, but kindly ensure to give my birthday party your full attention as soon as possible. It will be a huge event, simply an unforgettable one."

CHAPTER
TWELVE

"Because it's my birthday, Penelope, and because I am your sister, I mean your step-sister, would you please let me have a little ride on your horse? I do so want to and you did promise me," Sophie pleaded. Penelope smirked.

"Oh! please, Penny."

"How many times do I have to tell you, little girl, that my name is Penelope. I will answer to nothing less, particularly when it is when uttered through your lips."

"I am sorry, Penelope, but, please can I have a ride on Champion, just one, and I will never ask you for anything else."

"Well, I suppose it is your birthday, so... you will just have to wait and see. Will I let you have a ride on my Champion, or not? That, as they say, is the question and only I possess the answer to that particular query."

"Please don't tease, Pen...Penelope. Just one ride," she begged.

"What on earth is going on in here?" nanny, said, bursting into the room, with an armful of laundry.

"Nanny, will you *please* tell Penelope that she must let me have a little ride on Champion today? It is my birthday and I am three now."

"We are fully aware that it's your birthday, Miss Sophie, and I am quite sure that Miss Penelope will be only too pleased to indulge you," she said, rather loudly. Penelope completely ignored her.

"Do come along you two, no dilly-dallying, we all need to put our best foot forward. Guests will be arriving from two-thirty onwards. I will pop down to the kitchen to make sure that cook has everything in order. It is going to be a wonderful party. Now then, Miss Sophie, let me take those rags out of your hair before I go. You have the most beautiful, thick, black, hair, doesn't she, Miss Penelope? Mind you, your hair is just as lovely as your sister's, my dear," she wisely, added.

"Step-sister, nanny," Sophie, said. "Penelope has told me that I am her step-sister. I don't know what that means, do you? Does it make me more special than a sister?" Nanny didn't answer. It was Sophie's birthday and she was not about to spoil it.

For her part, Penelope had become skilled in the art of deception and, to all intents and purposes, and an untrained eye, she appeared to be a caring, even considerate, sibling, well step-sibling. A façade which fooled every one, apart from nanny, her very own poppa and her wicked step-mother, whom she hated with a vengeance.

Sadly, birthday or not, Sophie had no chance of ever putting her tiny foot into one of Champion's stirrups.

Penelope would never allow her to ride him but led her along, cruelly fuelling her desire to do so. Penelope did not know, nor want to learn, the meaning of sharing any of her possessions and that, as far as she was concerned, was the end of the matter.

"Miss Sophie, you are indeed every inch a princess," nanny said, tying the satin sash on her pink, party dress into a huge bow. Now, let me finish those ringlets off with these pink ribbons. You look beautiful, absolutely beautiful. That's it, give me a twirl. Oh! I almost forgot. A princess must have a tiara and this one is yours, at least for today," she said, placing a sparkly, tiny tiara onto her head.

"Thank you, nanny. I love my party dress," she said, spinning round whilst holding out both sides of the skirt.

"It is not me you need to be thanking, my dear. Everyone is waiting for you in the drawing room. Let's go down and show them how beautiful you are," she said, taking her hand and heading along the huge, galleried landing where they momentarily paused in front of the floor to ceiling mirror.

"Don't you look beautiful?" nanny, said.

"I am not quite as pretty as Penelope, am I? No one is, but I don't mind because I love her so much." Nanny pretended not to have heard Sophie's comment in response to her reflection. Had she dared to utter her thoughts she would have told Sophie that her innocence, her naivety, was far more beautiful than her stunning French silk, dress. It was not, however, nanny's place to verbalise such thoughts, although she often longed to set the record straight. Miss Penelope's feigned affection never pulled the wool over her weathered, wise eyes. She saw straight through her ugly, cruel game and gripped Sophie's hand more tightly.

"You are as pretty as a picture, Miss Sophie, and don't you ever doubt it," nanny said, as they made their way downstairs.

"Would everyone please be upstanding," nanny, said, opening the door to the drawing room, which was bursting at the seams with pink balloons, bubbles and perfectly-wrapped gifts.

"May I present, Miss Sophie, our birthday princess," nanny said. Everyone stood to attention and clapped with genuine delight as Sophie paraded around the room. Everyone, that is, apart from Penelope who turned her back on her family to look out through the window; a window not unlike the one in the hospital's discharge lounge. Sophie's birthday bubbles filled the room and floated around Penelope who took delight in bursting every one of them within her reach. Unable to resist her daughter a moment longer, Sophie's mother scooped her up in her arms.

"Thank you, Mummy. Thank you for my beautiful dress and ribbons," Sophie said.

"You will always be our princess, Sophie. We love you to the moon and back," her mother, said. "Sophie looks really beautiful, doesn't she, Penelope? Nanny has made a wonderful job of everything. Your sister looks beautiful, doesn't she, Penelope?"

"If you must know, I simply cannot abide all this fuss," Penelope said, pushing past her step-mother and sidling over to her father. Taking his hand, she said, "I would prefer to join you and the adults in the lounge, poppa, if you have no objection? I am far too grown-up for a little girl's party."

"Of course, you may join us," her father, said. "Nanny has made a splendid job of organising the party games and prizes. It is time we left the children to their fun," he said, taking his firstborn by the hand. "Let us retire to the lounge. I have uncorked a vintage bottle of port and may well allow you a little sip of it."

"You are not leaving me are you, mummy? Please stay." Sophie said.

"We will join you again before you blow out the candles on your scrumptious cake," she said, putting Sophie onto the floor. "Nanny, has made a splendid job of your party. Run along now and enjoy your fun and games. We will be here when you make a wish and blow your candles out. You must not tell nanny that I have told you this little secret, Sophie," she said, stooping down, "your cake has magical powers and when you blow out its candles, your wishes will all come true." Sophie's big, dark-brown, eyes, widened. "Now, enjoy your party games with your playmates. Poppa and I will be in the next room with Penelope and the grown-ups."

"I think the fog is beginning to lift," Penelope said, standing up to look through the window. "Oh, No! There she is again, skipping through the fog. Can you see her,

Frederick? You can see her, can't you? Her name is Sophie and she visits me in my dreams."

CHAPTER
THIRTEEN

"That's good news," Josie, the receptionist said, turning up the radio. "The fog has started to lift and traffic is moving, albeit slowly. Hopefully I will make my parley with Stan, at least it is looking more promising. I can almost taste a gin and tonic, served in a balloon glass with a sprig of mint and a striped straw," she quipped.

"Did you hear that?" Fred said. "The fog is lifting and hopefully we will all be on our way soon. Anyone care to join me outside for a quick nicotine break? What about you, Madame? he said. "Would you like to join me. Might do you good to stretch your legs."

"I would not venture into that fog if someone paid me to do so. Besides, I saw her, well, someone who reminded me of her out there. Whoever she was, she behaved like Sophie used to, skipping around everything. I ignored her then, years ago, and will continue to ignore any resemblance or reminder of her now. In my opinion, the weather forecast is incorrect. The fog may well be lifting in some areas, but it looks as dense out there as it was an hour ago. If one was not logically-minded, one may be tempted to assume that the fog, holding us captive, was being weighed down by images of one's past. Spectres that simply refuse to be silenced. But, one is logically-minded and therefore I refuse to accept or believe in anything supernatural. The fog is simply a natural phenomenon, nothing more."

"Oh! do give us all a break from your muttering, Madame?" Fred, said. "What about you, Sarah? Do you fancy joining me for a ciggie and a brew outside? Just a brew, if you are not addicted to nicotine."

"Thank you, Fred, but I prefer to wait inside. I do not want to miss my transport and I have no desire to relive my life. I do not need reminding of my mistakes."

"Would you like to join Frederick, Clarissa? I'm sure Sarah will watch your baby for you," Penelope, said.

"No offence, Penelope, but I have no intention of leaving my baby with anyone. We have all waited this long together so let's just sit it out. The fog is bound to clear soon. Why don't you try to relax, Fred? You know what they say, a watched kettle never boils and the time will not pass any quicker if you keep looking at the clock. It is rather like wishing your life away and I've done enough of that to last me a lifetime," Clarissa said, gazing into the fog which continued to taunt her.

"I've told you, Mum, I am not going to university even if they do offer me a place. My plans have changed, big time, and the sooner I get out of this house, the better," Clarissa said.

Her mother knew when she was beaten and, in resignation, watched her ambitions for her daughter's future hit the floor.

"When can we meet him then? This young man of yours. The one who has turned your head and apparently swept you off your feet."

"All in good time, mum. He will be worth the wait though, you'll see. I promise."

Clarissa was playing for time, postponing the reaction and repercussions of her decision.

That night she made her way to The Swan, their regular haunt, a hiding place of sorts. A place where they could be together without fear of reproach or retribution.

"You alright, Claris," Darren, asked. "Taking your time with that half of cider."

"Mum's been on her pedestal, lecturing me again, and, worse still, she is asking lots of questions about you. They want to meet you," she said, gripping the half-pint glass, more firmly.

"What's wrong with that? I would like to meet your parents. At least they would get to know me and realise that my intentions, as far as you are concerned, are honourable. They are Claris. You mean the world to me, honest, you do."

"But what if they don't accept you, accept us? What then?"

"Don't worry your little head about that. I can charm the back legs off a donkey and I will do just that. Charm my way into their hearts," he said, raising his pint pot to his lips. "Now get that cider down your neck. We have got the rest of our lives to plan and look forward to."

Darren was standing at the bar, chatting aimlessly to the landlord, busy pulling him another pint, when Clarissa's parents walked into the snug and made straight for the table where their daughter was staring into her half pint of cider.

"Where is he then?" her father, asked, "because you are not frequenting this establishment alone, are you? It is not a place for young ladies, well, respectable young ladies!"

Her mother stood alongside him, as upright as the street lamppost, illuminating 'The Swan' sign outside.

"How did you know I was here, dad?"

"It's a small village and those who live in it have got big mouths. Now where is he, this boyfriend of yours?"

"You must be Clarissa's father?" Darren said, stretching out his right arm to shake his hand. "You've timed it just right. Would you like to sit down and I'll get you both a drink. My treat."

"Your treat! I'll have you know that I will not be treated by you or any of your sort in a month of Sundays."

"Clarissa, get your coat. You are coming home with us, now!"

"I am not coming home, dad. I am staying here with Darren and you are welcome to join us. At least give him, us, the chance to talk to you. We would like to tell you about our plans."

"You'll have no plans, no future, with him," her father said, his face flushed, distorted. "Now get your coat, young lady and hope to God that no one has clocked you with him or you'll be ruined for life."

"I am not coming home, dad, and, do you know what I'm feeling right now? Ashamed. I am ashamed of you and your prejudice. I am staying here with Darren. I can understand why our relationship must have been a shock to you. A double whammy. But we love each other and what colour would you restrict love to? Answer me that one? Come on, mother. It's not like you not to have an opinion on any subject. What colour do you think love is, mother, dear?"

"Don't be so stupid. Love isn't a colour and it doesn't come sugar-coated either," her mother, said. "You are in for a rude awakening if you carry on like this."

"Love, sugar-coated or not, is not confined to a colour or creed. I'll have you know that the colour of our skin does not matter to us and it shouldn't matter to you, nor anyone else," Clarissa said. "Together, Darren and I are going to challenge the warped world we live in. Our love will demonstrate that there is a better way, a considerate way to stamp out prejudice and injustice."

"Over my dead body, will you be united with him, now get your coat. Do as you are told, now!" Clarissa's father, said.

"Do what your father tells you and get your coat," her mother, said. "You are coming home with us, where you belong, young lady, and your father is right. We can only hope that no one has put two-and-two together and if they have, they will think he was just a flash-in-the-pan. Fingers-crossed you haven't destroyed your reputation or you will live to regret your little fling."

"He is not a fling! He is my future, my everything," Clarissa, said.

"Please, sir. Just give me a moment. I beg you, sit down," Darren said.

"I will not sit down anywhere near you, ever. Now get your coat, Clarissa. We're out of here and he will never be welcome within a mile of our front door."

"Then you will walk out of here without me," Clarissa said. "I have made my choice and you have made yours."

"You silly girl. Do as you are told and get your coat, now!" her father, said.

"I am not coming dad unless you give Darren the chance he deserves. If not, you risk losing me, forever. The ball is in your court," Clarissa said, her words bouncing off the walls in the snug, yet icy-cold, room. Her parents were suspended, motionless and helpless in a defining moment in time they had not seen coming.

"The choice is yours, Clarissa, and yours alone. It is you who will lose everything," her father, said, resigning himself to the situation. "You have made your bed and I am afraid you will have to lie on it, however uncomfortable it proves to be. But, mark me well, my girl, having turned your back on us, you are no longer our daughter and you walk away wearing the clothes on your back, nothing more."

Aghast and shaken to the core, her parents made for the door, leaving their daughter destitute in the arms of her Caribbean boyfriend.

CHAPTER FOURTEEN

Fred stepped outside into the thick, swirling fog, lit a cigarette and closed his eyes. Almost immediately, an eeriness surrounded him, suffocating him, but there was no escape, no exit and sadly, no pause or delete button. Having lost his bearings and too afraid to open his eyes, he groped around searching for the hospital door, but it was gone and he was up to his ankles in mud and sludge.

Surrendering to his shadows of the past, Fred was in the thick of the battlefield, again, fighting in a war he had desperately tried to forget but which continued to torment him. He felt himself sinking into the filth and debris just as he had as a young, naïve soldier years before, when the screams and screeches of war had deafened and paralysed him. One cry, above all others, rang out loud and clear across the carnage; piercing, penetrating and muting every other sound.

"Come back, please don't leave me, Fred. Please don't leave me." There was no doubt who was calling his name, begging, pleading for his help. But Fred, the boyhood superhero, pretended not to hear his cries. There was no faithful Silver, his revamped set of pram wheels, waiting for the next delivery of newspapers he could utilise to aid their escape. No fearless Sampson, his first bicycle, to rescue him nor anyone else who could perch on the handlebars of his trusted steed. What's more, there was no one, in this hellhole, to sound the bugle charge or reveille call and there would be no eleventh-hour cavalry charge to save them. Childhood chivalry and feigned acts of courage he had watched on cinema screens and reenacted with his mates, were dead and buried in the mud, alongside the boys who had once played their innocent games, without a care in the world.

Fred threw his cigarette butt into the sludge, on top of the layer of filth and mire surrounding him, and started to wade through the blood-soaked, stinking field of corpses, dismembered body parts and foul debris, towards a wooded area. The smell of death and decay filled his nostrils. In his struggle, he left one of his boots, one of the very boots he had highly polished just a few weeks before, behind him, embedded in the mud. His other boot squelched as he yanked it free and started, slowly at first, to put one foot in front of the other, striding as far and as quickly as he could towards the wood, his perceived sanctuary, in a war-torn field. If he could cover the gulf between them, he would, he thought, be safe. He stumbled, not for the first time, face-down alongside comrades who lay wounded and dying. Caked in sludge, dripping with blood, he started to crawl, slithering over the top of every solid patch of ground he could grasp. His slow progress was hampered by the awful sensation of being buried alive, in a filthy open grave in no man's land. At such moments, almost of resignation, his thoughts turned to his mother and the pain his loss would cause her. She had warned him about the terrors of war and had been right about so many things which he had gullibly dismissed. In the thick of war's realities, the thought of her unbridled love, strengthened him. The nearer he got to the wood, the more subdued the gunfire became, but one cry, above all others, grew louder, reverberating through every fibre of his being.

"Don't leave me, Fred. Please don't leave me."

CHAPTER FIFTEEN

"Fred is still out there, somewhere," Penelope, said, glancing through the window. "One cannot help but wonder how many cigarettes he is getting through," she said, tutting and shaking her head, slightly. "There is no sign of him, not the faintest outline. This fog is relentless, unforgiving."

"Do sit down, Penelope, you are all of a shake," Clarissa said. "And, there is nothing out there, apart from fog and there is still plenty of that, regardless of what we have just been told. That receptionist needs to get her eyes tested if she thinks the fog is lifting because it hasn't budged an inch!"

I cannot rest, Clarissa. Although I am not one given to fanciful imagination, I did see my step-sister, Sophie, out there," Penelope said, nodding towards the window. "You do believe me, don't you, Clarissa?"

"To be honest, Penelope, I think staring into the fog is rather like gazing at the clouds floating across the sky. We can make all manner of shapes out of them, but we have to stare at them for an awfully long time before any of those shapes form pictures. Why don't you come and sit here for a little while and try to close your eyes, if only for a minute or two? At least Fred is giving us a break, even if he is contributing to the smoggy conditions."

"I know, without doubt, who it was I saw out there, my dear, so kindly refrain from patronising me," Penelope, said. "I may be old, but I am certainly not senile. Would you like to contribute to our discussion, Sarah? You have been rather quiet lately."

"What's the point?" Sarah, said. "If I am honest, very few people see any worth in the older population. So, why would they show any interest in anything we say or do? As we age we fade into the background if only to enable the next generation to take their place, it's the order of life. From my experience, however, too many retirees slowly disappear into nothingness, as they merge into the background of the communities they have loved and once served. We all reach a generational marker from which we start to disappear. It is logical progression, that is all.

"Did you say invisible?" Clarissa, said. "Because I know what invisible feels like and, I can assure you, that it is not something confined to one's age."

"Wait until you are my age, if you think you know how unimportant feels," Sarah said, her voice becoming bold and strong. "Believe me, every one of us will become surplus to requirements in a society which at best overlooks us, and at worst, ignores us. In my heyday, I was a top-class, stenographer. During the war years, I was responsible for creating the 'sorry for your loss' letters sent to unfortunate families to formally acknowledge their pain. Killed in the line of duty, and all that. I think I must have typed every letter to every wife, mother, father and family of those killed in combat, and who remembers their sacrifice or gives a hoot about them now? I've heard it said, more than once, that it is time to move on from the war-torn years, to stop looking back over our shoulders and erase the deaths, the casualties of war, forget them. But, that brigade can preach whatever they have a mind to because I, for one, will continue to acknowledge the sacrifice of those brave men and women. Acting respectfully costs nothing, but being overlooked and ignored, is detrimental and destructive. On the other hand, the thought of being patronised by do-gooders is even less palatable and much harder to stomach. Some of those goody-two-shoes peddle their own bikes in order to further their personal agendas and egos. Supporting us, after all, ticks a box on their Curriculum Vitae!"

"Well, if we weren't all feeling depressed before that little tirade, we certainly are now," Clarissa said. "Thank you, Sarah, but melancholia, given our situation, is unhelpful. The sooner we are discharged from here the better it will be for all of us. I have my whole life ahead of me and I intend to grab it with both hands and will do all in my power to ensure that Archie does as well. He is my future now," she said, cuddling her sleeping, baby boy.

"It is apparent, Sarah, that you are speaking from your own, very limited, experience," Penelope, said. "Your roots obviously lie in an unfortunate, somewhat unstable background. I, for one, strive to be a valuable member of the community, as do my cohort of associates, my peer group. One holds innumerable fundraising events for numberless worthy charities. Dinner parties are, without doubt, my forte and an absolute delight to organise. Then again, I belong to a rather refined circle of friends and regularly rub shoulders with dignitaries. Decorum is obviously in one's lifeblood, a calling, no less. Just between us, I have heard, via a reliable source, that I am in

101

line for a royal warrant, in acknowledgement of my services to the less fortunate," Penelope, said, fluttering her peacock feathers. "Perhaps royal recognition also equates to one's roots, one's social status and standing. Such credentials undoubtedly define one's value, regardless of one's age, in society. Surely, we must agree on that fact, my dear? Did you hear me, Sarah?" Penelope, said. Sarah shuffled on the high-backed recliner chair, lifted her head and looked Madame Penelope straight in the eye.

"I must agree, that aging undoubtedly has its advantages, but I have yet to discover precisely what they are," Sarah said, fixing her gaze on Penelope and resisting the temptation to ruffle her feathers too much. "We all have a battery life, Penelope, irrespective of the number of times we have been recharged and regardless of our backgrounds and upbringing. Even the health service categorises us according to our age. Decisions to treat a condition or allow nature to take its course, are made behind closed doors, based on our mental capacity or perceived lack of it. I admit that, at times, I have felt slightly confused and have, on occasions, had difficulty remembering dates and such like. And yet, on reflection, perhaps it is a kindness that I am not always conscious of my situation and the repercussions of the choices I have made. It is fair to say that some of life's decisions and detours were, undoubtedly, outside of my control. I was swept along on the tides of chance and, as a result, suffered its cruel consequences. We cannot compare ourselves as like with like, Penelope. My experience of aging is obviously very different to your own. Yet, I have always tried to do my best with the cards which life dealt me, even though those cards were rigged and stacked against me from the beginning and were certainly not the ones I would have chosen, had life been equal."

"I refuse to be distracted by gibberish and think it prudent to change the topic of conversation," Penelope, said. "One wonders if *you* have seen anything in the fog, Sarah? As I have already said, I am a practical and logical person and am inclined to believe that what I glimpsed was purely a figment of imagination. Afterall, my mind is far too astute to be tricked into thinking otherwise. But, have either of you seen anything out there? Well, have you?" she said, facing Sarah and Clarissa. "Kindly do me the courtesy of answering me. I must know the truth." None of the detainees answered her.

All three women, regardless of their age, upbringing and status, had seen images, visions of their past in the fog and this, if nothing else, united them. The room fell silent, apart from the sound of Josie's computer keyboard click, clicking behind the reception desk, piercing the stifled background noise of the radio. Penelope, having let her guard down a little too low, sought to backtrack.

"How long has Frederick been outside for?" she asked, peering through the full-length window, into the thickening, swirling, fog.

"There is no one from my past out there," Sarah said, standing up to join Penelope, at the window. But, no sooner had the words left her mouth than Sarah gasped, as she saw herself as the young woman she had once been, and, although she tried to close her eyes, if only to block-out the image, her gaze was fixed. The fog was closing-in on every

103

one of them, regardless of their status, or lack of it, and Sarah was no exception; none of them were.

CHAPTER SIXTEEN

Sarah had signed her flexible contract. There was little reason not to. Mr Davies was the perfect gentleman. Everything about him oozed class and the more she knew of him the more she warmed to his persona. Perhaps her life had turned around on a sixpence-of-chance and everything was knitting together into something beautiful, lasting. Despite her commitments, happiness was within her grasp and, for the briefest of moments, Sarah dared to believe that fate was shining a favourable light on her. Perhaps she had not been meant to accept the government job, after all. Her mother reminded her, time-and-again, that she was never to fret if she missed a bus because there would always be another one following in its tracks. Exercising patience in life's situations, became her tried and tested policy.

Sarah relished her flexible appointment at the bank almost as much, she liked to think, as the position she had allowed to slip through her fingers. Sadly, she knew the truth of the matter, even though she refused to admit it. A career in the halls of Westminster was the bus she had missed and another one, bound for the same destination, would never pass her way again. She comforted herself with the fact that she had fitted into the banking world, rather like a hand into a well-worn glove. Business lunches, shared with Mr Davies in up-market hotels, became regular appointments and ones she relished and looked forward to.

Having been singled out and treated to lunch, whilst being entertained by polite conversation, undoubtedly separated her from the rest of the administrative pack.

Looking out into the swirling fog, Sarah fixed her gaze, mesmerised, as she saw herself, as a young woman, being entertained by Mr Davies during one of their business lunches. This, she recognised, was the moment in time that revealed the flipside of fate's cruel sixpenny-bit of so-called chance.

Determined to face her skeletons, Sarah continued to watch the replay of another momentous turning point in her life. It was the point at which she realised that she had missed her opportunity of securing a successful career and a lucrative future, a decision she would rue for the rest of her life. Many years later, in a hospital discharge lounge, thoughts of boarding a train to London, Euston, still tormented her. She comforted herself by reiterating the fact that she had once been regarded as the best of a good bunch. Yet, on the day she declined a train ticket to London, she inadvertently settled for second-best and lived with the consequences of having done so. Hindsight was an indulgent, cruel pastime, fraught with regrets and merciless in its endeavours. There was no escaping the repercussions of missed opportunities.

"Well, Sarah, this is very pleasant, isn't it?" Mr Davies, said, reaching across the table and accidentally touching her red-painted, finger nails. "Sorry, my dear," he said, swiftly returning his hand to his wine glass. "Surely, you must realise that I have grown very fond of you. Immensely fond."

"I too enjoy and appreciate our lunchtime treats and am most grateful to you for the flexibility of the position I hold at the bank," Sarah said. William nodded, apprehensively running his finger around the top of his wine glass.

"Then allow me, despite my fear of rejection, to make a somewhat bolder suggestion, purely for your consideration, you understand. It is an arrangement which I hope will profit both of us, in somewhat rather different ways."

Mr Davies reached, more confidently, across the tablecloth, again. His rather sticky fingers deliberately lingered on her own, for which he displayed no embarrassment and made no apology for.

"You must realise, my dear, how much I respect, even revere you. In fact, I could while away the afternoon pouring out my admiration for you," he said, tenderly stroking her hand and looking her straight in the eye. "Yet, the time for small-talk is surely over, way behind us. You see, Sarah, my feelings for you run far deeper than esteem, respect and suchlike. I find myself no longer satisfied with a platonic friendship. I want to… well, enjoy more of you."

"Mr Davies, William, I…"

"Please, bear with me, my dear," he said, raising his hand. "I have no intention of ruining our relationship but rather enhancing it, consummating it, to be precise. Please allow me the courtesy of speaking freely to you about my feelings. Feelings which I sincerely hope, given time, will be reciprocated. Firstly, I must assure you that I will only ever regard you with the utmost reverence, your values will never be compromised. I am a very wealthy man, my dear, and if you accept my proposal you and your mother will want for nothing. I will take you both under my wing and shelter you from life's storms. You see, despite my success, I am a lonely man," he said, lifting his wine glass to his lips and dabbing the corners of his mouth with his white, starched napkin.

"Whilst I appreciate everything you have done for me, William, I cannot say that your feelings are reciprocated or that they ever will be. I am sorry. Please do not doubt that I will always be immensely grateful to you for the opportunities you have afforded me, but I do not find you attractive, at least not as a suitor, and my duty, you must understand, is to my mother."

"I do not expect you to love me, Sarah, but at least allow me the courtesy of explaining my arrangement to you in more detail. It is one which will comfortably provide for you and your mother. Surely, that alone, is sufficient incentive for you to consider my proposition in more detail, is it not? You will have your own home and you will both want for nothing. Do consider it carefully, my dear. You would be wise to weigh up the benefits of my proposal. Very wise, indeed."

"What exactly does 'comfortably provided for', mean, William? Are you asking me to marry you?" she said, pulling her hand away from his grasp. He smiled and sank back into his chair, caressing his glass of Beaujolais.

"I already have a wife, my dear. I am asking you to become my mistress and to bask in the luxuries that such a position would lavish upon you. Not forgetting, of course, the extensive benefits and security your mother would also be privy to. Caring for our nearest and dearest can prove extremely costly and yet they undoubtedly deserve the best we can afford them, do they not? Then again, the alternative to the offer may prove a rather awkward option and a hefty a price to pay. Let us put all of our cards onto the table, shall we? Now then, I think I am correct in assuming that your six-month flexible period of employment with us expires at the end of the month, does it not?

Sarah was not alone in the swirling shadows of the past. Fred, whom she could neither see nor hear, continued to battle with his own ghouls and ghosts.

CHAPTER
SEVENTEEN

Ignoring the cries for help billowing across the battlefield and bouncing off the clouds of war, Fred scrawled towards the wood, grasping at broken branches and tree trunks strewn across the perimeter of his perceived refuge. Finally, he curled up in the hollow of a huge oak tree, cupping his head in his bloodied hands. As night closed in around him, sounds and sensations became muffled as an unearthly quietness draped itself around him, lulling him to sleep in a false sense of security.

In the midst of war, Fred's dreams were of his boyhood. Having been deprived of a father's guidance, he forged his way through childhood and adolescence by playing the hero. Nonetheless, his memories were, in the main, happy ones, filled with escapades and adventures. In his dreams he sniggered at his fun-filled days and yearned to relive them, if only to experience the sheer joy and freedom they afforded him. How could that same young boy have imagined the horrors and realities of war which were suffocating and petrifying him now? Spinechilling squeals of fear and piercing screams of pain, anguish and loss had become his soulmates in a living nightmare. Numberless young men, boys at heart, lay dead and dying in the filth and debris of war. What were they fighting for anyway, freedom? In the midst of atrocious realities, he was learning, the hard way, that wars and rumours of wars, world wars no less, were indeed always on someone's agenda, somewhere. How he longed for peace and his carefree, childhood days and restful nights. He awoke from his slumber with a start, a cold fright. An owl, with piercing eyes and a shrill night cry, wakened him from his childhood dreams, as if calling him to attention.

"Come back, please don't leave me. Please don't leave me, Help," the wise owl seemed to screech, perched on a broken, oak branch, precariously positioned over the top of his blooded, bruised head. The owl's perceptive gaze penetrated his spirit, accusing and condemning him.

"The choice is yours, young man. Yours alone. Choose wisely, for you will live with the consequences of your decision for the rest of your days," it squawked, before disappearing into the night sky in search of its own prey.

Fred covered his ears, but the cries for help, awakened by the owl, would not be silenced. Even if he lost his ability to hear every other sound for the remainder of his life, he knew that he would always be tormented by the cries he had ignored. His dreams of boyhood, in which he had always played the caped hero, were over, yet, in the dead of night, at the centre of a bloody war, they raised their heads to challenge his fears and cowardice. Having reached a fork on the battlefield, his choice, from the ways before him, would shape his character for the rest of his life. Courage or cowardice? Right or wrong? Black or white? Life or death? Everlasting torment or eternal peace? Diametrically opposed values and their corresponding dangers and consequences, equally vied for attention, but there was only one path, one option available to Fred. It was time to resurrect his trusted Silver and faithful Samson. Time to find Billy, rescue him and bring him safely home. It was his defining moment in time.

CHAPTER EIGHTEEN

In the discharge lounge, Josie, the receptionist, made an announcement. "Good news, traffic is moving again, so that's a blessing and something we can all feel grateful for. Hopefully, the handovers will take place quite quickly now," she said, glancing at her watch.

"Have you heard the latest?" Stan, the porter, said, bursting through the doors.

"Just heard," Josie said. "Hopefully, all the discharges will be ticked-off soon and we'll make our date. What a day it's been! No two are alike though, are they?"

"We will only make our debrief if these four slow-coaches get a move on! I can't believe they are still here," Stan said, leaning over the reception desk.

"There's been more than the fog to contend with. Traffic has been at a standstill, but as I understand it, everything is moving again, so we just need this fog to clear. Sorry for the delay everyone."

"Did you hear that?" Clarissa whispered to her baby. "We'll be going home soon."

"Who is coming to collect you, Clarissa?" Sarah asked, looking at baby Archie.

113

"I'm not quite sure, but someone will."

"Not sure, my dear?" Penelope said, standing up to stretch her legs and exert her authority. "What about the child's father? Surely he will collect both of you."

If Clarissa heard Penelope's comment she did not respond but stood up to search the fog, hoping to catch a glimpse of her mother in its eeriness. Cuddling her own son and holding him tight, Clarissa finally realised how much her own mother had loved her. There was no doubt in Clarissa's mind that it was her mother who was standing at the bottom of her hospital bed when she had felt fearful. Mirage or not, it was, without doubt, her mother's love which strengthened her and enabled her to remain conscious and deliver her baby.

Sadly, when Clarissa's parents closed the door on the day they left their daughter with Darren in The Swan they lost everything they held dear, their most priceless possession. Ignorant of that truth, Clarissa and Darren faced a very different dilemma.

"What shall we do now? What will happen to us? Where can we go?" Clarissa, asked, searching Darren's face for a glimmer of reassurance. Her stance, although admirable, had not absorbed the full impact of her impulsive naivety and its lifelong repercussions. She had thrown a huge boulder into the lake of prejudice and its ripples, its tidal waves, were about to overwhelm them. Surely her parents would be won over to her way of thinking? It was clearcut. Prejudice was evil. Besides, who could not love Darren? He was a wonderful man, a man with prospects, who was going to smash the ceiling of prejudice and injustice. But, what if her parents did not come round to her perspective, her way of thinking? What would become of her? She knew, without doubt, that she was right in her stance against prejudice, but how much would that cost her and would it be worth losing her family for? Darren did love her, didn't he? He was reliable, wasn't he?

An uncomfortable silence hovered over their small, round table in The Swan, smothering them in the not-so-cosy, snug. Everything had changed, shifted in one defining moment of time.

"Don't worry, Clarissa, my love. Your parents will accept me. They will have to because we won't be beaten, will we?"

"You heard what my father said. I only have the clothes on my back and I cannot ask them for a penny. To be honest, I wouldn't stoop to ask them for anything. I'm not a beggar but, then again, I haven't got anything to call my own. Where can I go, Darren? Where can we go?"

"Penny for your thoughts, Clarissa?" Sarah said, sensing the heaviness surrounding the young mother and her baby.

"We can't escape our past, can we, Sarah? None of us can and if we try to, it chases after us." Clarissa said. "As painful and unpleasant as it may be, the past finds a way of catching up with us, overtaking us, when we least expect it. I really miss my mum. I just wish she could have seen baby Archie. She would have loved him. My mum's father, my grandfather, was an Archibald, a good, hard-working man.

115

Mind you, he regularly downed more than a pint, or two of best bitter, but he was a generous-hearted soul. Archie is a name to be proud of and one which means genuine, bold and brave. Something to live up to, my son," Clarissa, whispered to him.

"Archibald is more far more refined than Archie, my dear," Penelope, said. "Perhaps you will consider addressing him more formally in future, particularly in more salubrious settings."

"Thank you, Penelope, but I prefer Archie. I don't care for status. From my experience the world is a cruel, selfish place and Archie will need to be bold and brave to succeed in it and that is the advice I will be giving him. I will advise him not to run with the pack and to swim against the tide, upstream, if he needs to, especially in his fight for truth and justice. He will have to be strong to fight prejudice in its many forms. It's pure evil."

"One can appreciate your rather naïve sentiment," Penelope, said. "In fact, no one has been braver than my own son in such matters. Edward is dignified, refined in every respect and selective in his choice of friends and associates, unquestionably upper-class. He stands head and shoulders above society's bravest and best and he is indebted to no man."

"I take it Edward is your only child," Sarah said.

"Of course, my dear. As soon as my husband and I had a son, an heir to our estate, our lives were complete."

"Were you an only child, Penelope?"

"I was but… but, then again, not really. I had a step-sister. Her name was Sophie, but she was ***not*** my sister."

If Madame Penelope thought she would escape her own past being replayed in the swirling fog simply because she refused to believe it, then she was mistaken. Closing her eyes, her mind, her heart, to all thoughts of the past, she fell asleep into a nightmare of unjustifiable events.

*****

"This is a wonderful birthday party, isn't it, Penny?" Sophie, her step-sister, said, skipping around her in the dining room.

"What did you call me? How many times do I have to tell you? My name is Penelope and you are ***not*** my sister. Kindly address me formally and never overlook the fact that our relationship has been forced upon me. Today may be your birthday, ***little one***, but it is just another day in my book. Nothing special and I would suggest you endeavour to enjoy it whilst it lasts. Life will revert to normal as soon as the clock strikes midnight."

"Oh, I will enjoy it, Penelope, especially if you play the games with me. You promised you would."

"I did not promise anything of the sort. One feels rather tired today," she said, feigning a yawn. "Now run along and play pass-the-parcel and blind man's bluff with nanny and your playmates. I am going to have a little rest. That sip of port has left me feeling rather tired."

117

"Well, will you please let me have a ride on Champion after you have had a rest?"

"Did I not make myself perfectly clear? He is *my* Champion, mine and mine alone, and he does not like little girls wearing party dresses. In fact, he detests them."

"I'll take my party dress off, then," Sophie, said, pulling at her tiara, firmly clipped into her ringlets.

"Very well, I will consider it," Penelope said, looking over her shoulder, as she made her way towards the dining room door.

"You are not leaving us, are you, Miss Penelope?" nanny, said. "It is your sister's birthday and she is really looking forward to sharing her party games with you. It will mean the world to her. Do stay."

"I am *not* staying for one minute longer than I have to. Allow me to spell it out for you, nanny. I am not in the slightest bit interested in anything associated with my step-sister, birthday girl or not. Is that clear?"

"It is Sophie's birthday and you are her big sister. She looks up to you, admires you, only God knows why she does, though!"

"What did you say? How dare you! Remember your place, nanny. One word in my poppa's ear will bring about your demise. I suggest that you know your place and remain in it. And you, of all people, know that she is not my sister and her mother is not my mother and my poppa is my poppa, mine, not hers!"

"I beg your pardon, Miss Penelope," nanny said, bobbing her knee. "I will endeavour to entertain Miss Sophie and her friends, although she will be very disappointed if you do not join her. Surely, it is not too much to ask. Perhaps think of it as a birthday treat for her and one she will always remember."

Penelope smirked. "I am confident, nanny, that you will more than compensate for my absence which, after all, is what poppa pays you to do, is it not? One does not keep a dog and bark oneself."

Penelope's entire body twitched as she awoke with a start in the hospital chair in the discharge lounge.

"Are you alright, Penelope?" Sarah asked. "Were you day-dreaming?"

"One could say that, but it was more akin to a nightmare than a dream, although it is one I am accustomed to."

"Would someone open one of those double-doors for me, please?" Sarah said. "I need some fresh air."

"Surely, you are not thinking of going outside, are you?" Clarissa said. "It is still rather foggy. Besides, Fred is out there somewhere, no doubt smoking his head off!"

"I just need some fresh air. Please open the door. I won't step too far into the fog."

Against her better judgement, Clarissa opened the door. Sarah gingerly stepped over its threshold and immediately disappeared into the shadows of her past.

CHAPTER NINETEEN

"Do you think one of us should join Sarah outside?" Clarissa asked, turning to Penelope. "She didn't seem very steady on her feet to me."

"Absolutely not," Penelope, said. "She foolishly chose to venture outside and who I am, or anyone else for that matter, to show an ounce of concern for an old fool's, puerile decision. Besides, Frederick, another well-oiled joker, is still roaming around out there. Hopefully Sarah will cross paths with him, join forces, so to speak. Who on earth, in their right mind, would want to stand out there inhaling smog? It certainly reveals the level of one's intelligence, or lack of it, to do so!"

"Well, do you think the images we have seen in the fog, are real or simply figments of our imagination, Penelope?" Clarissa, asked.

"Do let us remain logically minded, Clarissa. We are all rather tired, and longing for home comforts. It is so very stuffy in here and I simply refuse to be perturbed by anything I may, or may not, have seen. I regularly see a little girl in my dreams but that is something I simply choose to ignore. Compartmentalising one's experiences is a worthwhile, prudent exercise."

"Do you know who the little girl is and why she features in your dreams?" Clarissa said, glancing through the window.

"As I have already explained to you, I do not entertain spectres," Penelope, said. "Our minds enjoy tricking us, particularly in stressful situations. The time we have spent together in here has been extremely tense and appears to have taken its toll on all of us, in one way or another. Enough of this topic. That little boy of yours is such a good baby."

"It is not Archie I feel concerned about, Penelope. It is the eeriness of our situation. Have you never caught a glimpse of someone out of the corner of your eye, only to realise that no one is there? Or sensed a presence alongside you during the most difficult times of your life? I know I have, especially when I was giving birth to Archie," she said, holding him up over her left shoulder. I thought, for the briefest moment, that I saw my mother standing at the foot of my hospital bed. I admit that I was racked in pain and haemorrhaging quite heavily at the time and everything in the room was blurred, hazy. Nevertheless, I thought that I glimpsed her. Then again, it could not have been her," she said, reaching into her pocket to make sure that the letter it contained was safe.

"Of course, it could not have been your mother," Penelope, said. "You have answered your own anomaly. You were haemorrhaging and your brain was starved of oxygen. It can be explained away as simply as that. You would be well advised never to read too much into those silly experiences; stuff and nonsense."

122

"But it is said that the dead do not completely disappear from our lives as long as we remember them and that they find their place and purpose in our recollections. You see, Penelope, I received this letter a few weeks before Archie's due date, informing me that my mother had passed away," she said, placing the contents of her pocket and a crumpled, envelope containing a well-read piece of paper, onto the chair next to Penelope.

"That must have been a terrible shock for you, Clarissa, particularly the timing of it," Penelope said, refusing to acknowledge the letter. "It is quite understandable that, in your hour of need, you imagined that you saw your mother. But, it is entirely illogical and you would do well to adjust to life's gains and losses, sooner rather than later. Forget the past and those who have gone before and focus your time, attention and energies on young Archibald. I did exactly that when I chose to forget my life's hiccups and channelled my efforts into more prosperous endeavours. Edward, is indeed a son to be proud of and one who has risen to the very top of society and is indebted to no man. He is awfully handsome and is married to a well-educated lady, of considerable standing. It is vitally important to have prospects, my dear, and it is never too late to aspire to them. I am confident that Edward will be the first person to arrive here," she said, buttoning her coat up, again. "I just need to be ready to fly. He barely has a minute to spare these days. Mind you, I too have little time or incentive for day-dreaming. Business is paramount."

"I don't mind telling you, Penelope, that the things I thought I saw out there, in the fog, distressed me," Clarissa said, nodding towards the window. "Not that what I saw wasn't true, because it was, all of it. But, seeing it replayed

123

before my eyes was sad, to say the least, especially in the light of my mother's death. You see, we did not make our peace with each other before she passed away. I had the opportunity to do so, but I didn't take it. My pride would not let me. I thought there would always be tomorrow and that is where I was mistaken. I wish I had swallowed my pride and seized the moment. It is often said, that as we age, the only things we regret in life are the things we do not do or do not say when given the opportunity to do so. Perhaps it was my mother I saw standing at the bottom of my bed, willing me to fight, to live. I wonder if we can still ask those who have passed away to forgive us? Is it ever too late to apologise and to say we are sorry to those we have hurt, inadvertently or deliberately?"

"Apologies are for the weak-willed and minded, my dear. One must stand by the decisions one makes throughout life, whatever their consequences may be. Non desideriis, my dear, no regrets and certainly no apologies."

"I just wish my mum had been able to see her grandson and hold him in her arms. Then again, knowing mum, she would probably have whispered a blessing over him, although blessed is the last thing I feel at the moment. Nothing has worked out for me as I would have liked it to. But, life will be different for you, Archie, I promise you it will, and I will do everything in my power to make it a bed of roses for you," she said, cuddling her baby boy close to her heart.

"One has to make the most of this life, Clarissa. Grasp every opportunity presented to us with both hands. That is my philosophy, my rule-of-thumb, and if one does not adhere to that, then one only has oneself to blame for missing the boat, so to speak."

Clarissa did not hear Penelope's comment. Despite life's disappointments she felt thankful for the unspeakable gift of her baby son.

"Someone will come for us soon, my boy. I am not quite sure who that someone will be, but they will come for us and I promise you that we will live happily, ever after."

"I am sorry I cannot take you home with me, Clarissa," Darren said, over the table in The Swan. "Honestly, Claris, there isn't any room for you where I come from. We are crammed-in as it is and I haven't told my mother about us, yet. To be honest, I'm not sure what her reaction will be when I do pluck up the courage to tell her, especially after your parents made their feelings about us quite clear."

"But, we are going to take on the world's prejudice and change it, beat it into submission, aren't we? Clarissa, said. We are going to prove them all wrong. Our love is going to challenge prejudice and win," she said.

Darren placed one of his strong arms around her.

"My love, my innocent, beautiful love. You have no idea of the height, depth and power of the barriers of injustice and prejudice we face. We are ahead of the times, ahead of our time. There has to be a united shift in society, a very big one. Wrongs and injustices have to be righted but, on the other hand, change takes time and you, my lovely girl, are far too delicate, too naïve, to weather such

125

storms. In fact, I should have known better than to have fallen for your smile, your innocence."

"You underestimate me, Darren. I am up for the fight, honestly, I am. Please introduce me to your family. We can tell them of our plans for our future together. I will sleep on their sofa if they will let me. They will not even notice I am there. I promise to be as quiet as a tiny dormouse."

"That is out of the question, Claris. It is definitely not an option. Honestly, there isn't any room, even for a little one, at our house and my family's heart is not ready to welcome you or anyone else. Truth is, my mother has set her sights on a girl who sings in the gospel choir to hook me up with, but as nice as she is, she isn't you and it's you I love. Try not to worry, we will find a way through this mess. I will look for a place for us to live and, in the meantime, you could try the local council, perhaps they can offer you something. I'm pretty sure they've got somewhere available for people in your situation, emergency accommodation for the homeless, that sort of thing. At least you fit into that category, don't you?"

"Homeless! Emergency accommodation! Are you joking, having a laugh?"

"I'm sorry, Claris. I should have said for people like us. Thinking about it, perhaps it might be worth going back to live with your parents, just for a little while. Play the game a bit to buy us some time until we get a roof over our heads."

"I will never go back there, Darren. My parents are bigots and I am ashamed of them. Besides, I will not give them the satisfaction of crawling home with my tail between my legs. I want them to get the message that I mean what I say and it's my life and I can do whatever I like with it. I'm sick of being suffocated."

"I understand how you feel and I don't blame you. I'm sorry, Claris. Thing is, I dare bet that my family, like yours, will have similar feelings about us being an item, especially because my mother has a nice girl in mind for me. But, don't worry, we will find a place where we can be together. A place where we can build a home and raise a family. You do want a family, don't you?"

"Of course, I do, and…"

"But what about your dreams of college, university and a professional career. You are a bright girl, a shining star, and I don't want to be the one who clips your wings. You, my love, were meant to soar."

"What dreams? I only dream of you now, Darren and being together and… and…"

"And what?"

"And the baby, our baby, this baby," Clarissa said, stroking her belly.

"Pregnant! You can't be, can you? Are you sure? We've been really careful. Bet you're just running late with all the fuss your parents have kicked up. It's not surprising you're overdue, is it?"

"I am not overdue, I am quite sure, Darren. I have had a pregnancy test and it's positive. It's not about me now, it's about us and the baby. I have relinquished my dreams of university and a career. They were pie in the sky, anyway. You and our baby are my priority now. Come on, let's make our way to the council offices. They can't turn me away, especially in my condition, and if they do I will camp out on their front steps until they find somewhere for me, for us, to live."

CHAPTER TWENTY

"I'm tired of staring at the four walls of this waiting room," Clarissa, said. "Would you like to pass the time by telling me about the little girl, Penelope, the one with ringlets in her hair? It would occupy our minds."

"I refuse to share my recollections of that girl with you or anyone else and kindly show me the courtesy of not referring to her again. I do not believe in looking back over one's shoulder." Penelope said, walking towards the window. "Now what, I wonder, is happening to Sarah out there?"

"I cannot believe my own ears, William? "Would you honestly not renew my employment contract if I decline your offer to become your concubine?" Sarah, said, folding her napkin before standing up to leave the table.

"I would not do that, Sarah. I would never do that! You misjudge me and my motive. Please sit down and allow me explain."

"What did you mean, if not exactly that? Threatening me with the termination my employment at the bank," she said, teetering on the edge of her chair.

"It was not a threat. I would never threaten you. My bargain is this, if you accept the offer on the table, you would not need to work again, unless you desire to do so. Every one of your needs, and those associated with caring for your mother, would be met under the terms of our agreement."

Sarah sighed and repositioned herself in the plush, dining chair. Had she misjudged the man and been fooled by his demeanour and taken for a ride? The façade was over, the game was up and William was tripping over his halo. He was anything but Mr Boring Average Man, so labelled by the bank's gullible employees. Who could have seen what lay underneath his mask, behind his spick-and-span appearance, his pinstriped suit and matching shirt and tie? And yet, Sarah realised that she must not be hasty in her response before learning the facts, figures and red tape contained in the offer. She owed it, not least to her mother, to pragmatically consider her position and William's proposition. Their home was far from comfortable and, having allowed one golden offer to slip through her fingers, she sat back in the chair and beckoned to the waiter to fill her wine glass. Perhaps she had been too hasty in her judgement of his proposal.

"I would obviously need to read the fine print contained in such an agreement, Mr Davies," she said, raising the glass to her lips. He sat back and smiled. She was on his hook and he would relish reeling her in and confining her to his keepnet.

Penelope, stood up to peer through the window, scanning the density of the fog for a vague outline of Sarah

130

but her feet became rooted to the spot. She was captivated, spellbound and unable to move a muscle in order to escape the images of her past.

"Please, not here. Not now," Penelope, said. "Besides, such visions are simply a result of dehydration, or an adverse reaction to medication. That is all you are and I will never believe otherwise," she said. But it was too late. The day Penelope had endeavoured to erase from her consciousness for a lifetime had started to replay and there was no escaping it.

Penelope was being forced to face her own ghosts by continuing to watch a rerun of her step-sister's birthday and the part she had played in it. A force, stronger than autonomy, was controlling her and, as uncomfortable as it was, she had no alternative other than to relive the day.

"I am so excited, nanny," Sophie said, twirling around the room in her party dress and silver tiara which highlighted her jet-black hair and huge, dark brown, eyes.

"Well, we have got a lot of games to play today," nanny, said, "and, I wonder who will win all of those prizes? Come along now, I have just heard the doorbell. Your friends must have started to arrive," she said, taking Sophie's tiny hand in her own.

Penelope grimaced as she watched Sophie twirling around and clapping her hands. Her step-sister was nothing more to her than a puerile nuisance, an unpleasant, unwanted bee, in a jar of luscious honey. Penelope had always detested Sophie and always would. The passing of

131

time had not softened the hard, cruel resentment she harboured towards her. Why, oh why, did Sophie have to spoil everything? And why did her poppa have to marry her ugly, step-mother? They had spoilt everything and ruined her life.

Penelope had always been the apple of her poppa's eye and her father's love had, in many ways, compensated for the loss of her mother. Penelope's security, rooted in her poppa's love, was destroyed when, on the winds of chance and change, her step-mother appeared, quite unexpectedly, on the scene. Little did she know that Penelope would never share her father, whom she was petrified of losing, with anyone, especially a selfish, step-mother and a silly, stupid step-sister.

Unable to close her eyes to the scene, Penelope continued to sneer at every boring game she had refused to partake in. Being forced to watch giggling children, overreacting with shouts and shrieks of excitement, running around the room in a game of musical chairs, was painful. It was all so unrefined and undignified. Penelope tried again, in vain, to look away, but she was fixed to the spot.

"Nanny where is Penelope?" Sophie, asked."

"I have told you, Miss Sophie. Penelope is very tired but she is hoping to join us a little later. Why don't we go outside, onto the lawn, and play Blind Man's Bluff? That is always fun."

The children screeched and danced around the dining room while nanny unlocked the French doors onto the lawn.

"Yippee! Penelope, will be coming to play with us soon," Sophie shouted to her playmates, although no one heard her.

"Come along now, sit down on the grass, while I sort the blindfold out for our next game. Look, Miss Sophie, it's a pretty pink blindfold to match your dress. Let me straighten your tiara and tidy up those ringlets of yours. You will really enjoy Blind Man's Bluff and because it's your birthday, you will be the first one to wear the blindfold and try to catch one of your friends."

Glued to the scene, Penelope could not move a muscle as images of the day, and the part she had played in it, continued to unwind.

"Nanny, poppa needs you in the lounge *immediately*," Penelope called, ignoring every one of the children, especially Sophie.

"Now!" Nanny said, scanning the fifteen, excited children, who were refusing to stand still.

"Yes, that is correct, nanny. Immediately," Penelope said.

"Very well. But you will have to keep an eye on the children for me. We were just about to play Blind Man's Bluff."

"Oh! do I have to?" Penelope, who could think of nothing worse to do, said.

"Well, you are the only other person available and it is your sister's birthday. So do pardon me, Miss Penelope, but surely it is not too much to ask, is it now?"

"Careful, nanny. Kindly remember who you are addressing. And, surely I do not need to remind you that Sophie is *not* my sister," Penelope said, as she sidled towards the cacophony of children.

"Please stay, Penny," Sophie said. "Look everyone, this is my big sister, Penelope," she quickly added, in response to the look on her step-sister's face.

"Very well, if needs must, nanny" Penelope said, looking over her shoulder. "But kindly ensure to return in double-quick time or one may be tempted to leave the little treasures to their own devices."

CHAPTER
TWENTY-ONE

Josie, the receptionist, was busy sorting through the case notes ensuring that everything was ticked off when the door squeaked open and Stan, peered around the door.

"Sorry about this, Miss Woodridge," he said. "But I am running a bit late. There is a huge backlog in A&E and I am doing all I can to help the situation."

"Does that mean our get-together is off?" Josie, said, because that is the last thing I want to hear! I could really do with a heart-to-heart after today."

"It's definitely not off. It would take more than a bit of fog and a huge backlog to do that. It just means that our downtime might happen a little later than we planned. I have been chasing my tail all day but I don't seem to be getting very far. I've felt a bit on the fringe of things. No doubt we will make up for lost time, later, if you catch my drift. In fact, I'll make sure we do," he said, striding towards the desk.

"Hope so. I thought there was a glimmer of light at the end of the foggy tunnel and we had finally turned a corner in our mission, especially since transport is moving again," she said, "but, then again, you know what they say, 'don't count your chickens before they hatch'. I'm thankful for small mercies, nonetheless."

"Nothing else for it," Stan said. The world won't stop turning because we've got a hot date neither of us want to miss."

"Less of the hot, if you don't mind, Stanley."

"Well, you are such a sweetie and you don't half bring out the best in me!" he said, smirking.

"That crass comment has just cost you a double, which I will be downing in one, providing everything goes to plan. And, whatever you do, please don't wheel any last-minute trollies through that door. I have had more than my share of them today and am finding it difficult not to absorb their emotions and soak up some of their pain. If I'm not careful, it takes the shine off everything else. I know I shouldn't, but I've just been reading through one of their stories," she whispered, tapping a set of case notes. It's so sad."

"I've heard more than my share of sad stories as well, too many to number, if I'm honest. I try my best to switch off to them, but, then again, I like to think that I'm shining a bit of light in the darkness. Let's face it, folk wouldn't be in here if they weren't suffering, would they? Talking of which, I thought there was four, awaiting discharge? I can only see two. Where are the others, especially Frederick, the trouble-maker? He hasn't tried to do a runner, has he?" Stan said, looking around the waiting area. "Thing is, he won't get very far, if he has, given the weather."

"Keep your voice down, Stanley. I think Fred has stepped outside, probably for a cigarette," Josie said, "and Sarah, one of the others, has joined him. I don't think she's

136

a smoker though, not that that matters. I think it's a step closer to home for both of them."

Fred was a million miles away from the confines of the hospital, absorbed in the replay of the worst of his days. He was running, as fast as his legs would carry him, across the war-torn trenches, towards the spot where he had left Billy wounded and unable to move. In his blinkered determination to find his friend, Fred did not feel his remaining boot leave his foot. Even if he had, he would not have stopped to rescue it, for fear of the temptation to turn on his one and only heel and run away. In a blind panic, gasping for breath, he ran towards a breach in the field, close to his infantry. Thick smoke and the stench of death and dying filled his nostrils, stinging his eyes and limiting his vision. He started to stumble again, tripping over dismembered corpses, in a frenzy of blind panic. Falling to his knees, he started to scream and shout his head off, as tears streamed down his battered, bloodied face. No one acknowledged him, because no one heard his cries above the sounds of war.

"Dear God," Fred sobbed, "don't desert me in this hellhole. If you're there, please help me find Billy." An eerie, blanketed hush covered the battlefield. Every movement, every cry became subdued, stunted and surreal, apart from that of Billy's, which rang out loud and clear.

"Over here, Fred. I'm here," he shouted. It was the only voice Fred heard in answer to his prayer. That he was barefooted, bloodied and bruised was of little consequence. He felt no pain or discomfort. Billy was alive and although Fred's heroic cape was invisible to the naked eye, it was,

137

nonetheless, firmly fastened around his neck, flying behind him in a blaze of glory as he ran towards his lifelong friend.

"There you are, Billy," he said, falling to his knees.

"I knew you would come back for me, Fred. I knew you wouldn't leave me to die in this filth, on my own. I would have put money on you saving me. You have never let me down, not once."

"That's enough of that talk. We are getting out of this together and what's more, we will live to tell the tale to our grandkids," he said, glancing at Billy's injuries whilst surveying the situation. At that unearthly moment, however, fear, from nowhere, swamped him and started to whisper its lies in his ear. 'Who are you trying to kid, Fred? You are a coward and you are both as good as dead. The only place you pair will be going is six-foot under. There's a trench over there with your names on it.' Fear's taunts were, in part, true and yet, from somewhere beyond its realm of power, Fred found the courage to ignore its intimidation and lies. He had, after all, heard them all before.

Fully aware of the reality of his situation, Billy reached up and touched Fred's face with his fingertips. "It's ok, mate. You came back for me and that is all that matters. I didn't want to bleed to death on my own," he said, forcing Fred to look him in the eye.

"We're not done yet, Billy," Fred said, scanning the battlefield. "Stay with me; look at me; focus and press this on your gut," he said, taking a scarf, of sorts, from around

138

his neck. "Your number's not been called and it's not your time. The only place you are going, is home."

"I can't move a muscle, Fred. I'm done for, on my way out. Leave me be and save yourself," Billy said, pressing the cloth over his wound.

"We are leaving here together or not at all. I'll find a way through, I always have," he said, scanning the field. "Well, I never, there she is and that will do very nicely! If it isn't Silver Mark2! Better than any faithful steed," Fred said. Scrawling across the top of the bloodbath he grasped the handles of a makeshift wheelbarrow and dragged it back to where Billy lay.

"Don't tell me you are thinking of putting me into that thing; Silver Mark2 or not! I served my time, playing dead, on Mark1, remember, so no more fun and games. Spare a dying man that much!" he chuckled, blood splurging from the corners of his mouth.

"I am taking you home, Billy on Silver Mark2, the best mode of transport in the world. No expense spared for you, my mate, and it won't be the first time you've rode on a trolley of sorts, or sat on a pair of handlebars, will it? And, this time, you won't have to pretend to be Guy Fawkes, and I won't be begging for money off folk for fireworks and bangers. We've heard and seen enough explosions and carnage in this place to last us both a lifetime. I just need to get you into this little beauty," he said, placing one arm underneath his playmate's head.

139

"You're hurting me, Fred. Please don't try to move me, I'll bleed out. I'm not going to make it," he said, covering his body with his bloodied, dirty hands.

"Here, press this on it," Fred said, starting to unbutton his jacket."

"It's no use, Fred. You have to leave me where I fell. You've got to. It's enough that you came back for me," he said, gripping Fred's tattered coat sleeve in an attempt to stop him from taking his coat off. But it was too late. Fred was on a mission.

"I am not leaving you, Billy, so bite on this," he said, placing a piece of wood in his mouth, "and hold my jacket on that wound. I'm taking you home."

Sarah was also reliving her past and had succumbed to William's cohabitation offer, if only to provide the comforts her mother deserved. At least, under William's roof, they would both have their own privacy, which was just as well, since William could arrive on any day, at any time. Although Sarah would never fully recover from life's disappointments they had taught her to make the most of every opportunity and to never look a gift horse in the mouth. As for William, he more than kept his part of the bargain and lavished every home comfort imaginable upon her. On occasions, Sarah pretended that they were a happily married couple who had built a home together, but the fallacy quickly evaporated when William left her to be with his wife and children. Sarah had no set times for their get-togethers and was required to be ready and waiting for William's visitations at any hour of the day or night. He owned and subtly controlled her. Her mother, quite unexpectedly, wallowed in the comforts that her daughter's sacrifice had secured for them. Over time, she regained a modicum of health and discovered a renewed vitality for life, which warmed Sarah's heart. She had made the right decision and, in so doing, had given her mother a second-innings, an innings she more than deserved.

"Where are you off today, mum, dressed to kill?" Sarah cheerily, asked.

"I'm going down to the social club at the end of the road. It's a friendly bunch and we don't half have a laugh, which lifts our spirits. We call ourselves the little group of merry widows and let our hair down a bit, when no one is looking, of course. I owe every ounce of my happiness to your good fortune, Sarah. Fate smiled on us the day you met William, didn't it? He is such a good man, isn't he and you are happy with the arrangement, aren't you?"

"I am as happy as one can be given the circumstances, mum. Please don't concern yourself about me. I can play the game to perfection. William is a good man, kind-hearted, if misunderstood by his associates. We never saw a life of luxury and good fortune coming our way, did we? Life is truly worth living now and I am grateful that you are feeling and looking so much better. God knows, we have weathered our fair share of storms, but the wind is in our sails now, and it's onwards and upwards. We have everything to live for and it's time to start counting our blessings."

Unfortunately, at the beginning of what started as a quiet, sun-filled morning, everything, before the sun set, would be turned upside down and Sarah would be faced with another defining moment.

"I'm just popping out, Mum, I won't be long.

CHAPTER
TWENTY-TWO

Back in the discharge lounge, Clarissa was pacing the floor, cuddling baby Archie, in her arms.

"Do sit down, Clarissa," Penelope said.

"I will only sit down if you tell me what happened to your step-sister,"

"I am not one for sharing personal information, Clarissa, despite its popularity. Perhaps the aim of such theories is to reconcile one's past in order to move forward, on the premise of another mantra. I can, of course, appreciate why therapies are portrayed as a remedy, of sorts, for life's trials and tribulations. But, surely one is entitled to adopt one's preferred strategies when facing life's hurdles and disappointments. In keeping with society's elite, I was raised to adopt a stiff upper lip approach and quickly learned the technique of bury one's feelings and... and... oh no! Look, Clarissa, look into the fog. That little girl is Sophie, my step-sister," Penelope said, standing up and walking, unsteadily, towards the patio doors.

"Please excuse me, Clarissa. One's past can threaten to overtake even the best of us and I refuse to allow it to intimidate me. I have seen regret stalk its prey many times and I refuse to be hunted by it. I will never become its victim. Kindly excuse me, my dear, I need to step outside to confront the spectre and confirm that she is purely a figment of imagination. Besides, it is rather stuffy in here and I need to stretch my legs. I will prove, beyond doubt, that Sophie is nothing more than an illusion and one that will dissipate into the fog, when challenged."

Before Clarissa could deter or dissuade her, Penelope stepped outside and disappeared into the past where her stiff upper lip would be challenged.

Penelope watched nanny hurry towards the dining room in response to Lord Cuthbertson's request for assistance.

"In my absence, please be kind enough to oversee the fun and ensure that the children are entertained. They have been enjoying the party games, so please do not spoil their fun. We were just about to play Blind Man's Bluff," nanny said. Penelope ignored her.

Sophie's eyes were blindfolded and she was trying, albeit unsuccessfully, to catch one of her playmates, who were taunting her with shouts of 'I'm here' whilst running round every inch of the patio.

"Stop! Stop it at once and stand still, immediately," Penelope shouted. "That is quite enough squealing and giggling. Sophie, stand still," she commanded, grabbing her step-sister's shoulders and pulling the mask up and over the top of her head. Her playmates stiffened as though suspended in a game of frozen statues, apart from Sophie, who looked lovingly into her big sister's eyes.

"What are we going to play, now?" she asked, gasping for breath and pulling at Penelope's dress. Her playmates joined the chorus, echoing her plea. Sophie was overjoyed. Her big sister had joined her party and she was far too excited and naïve to notice a flaw or threat in her persona. Every child, especially Sophie, was at Penelope's mercy and she was about to tighten her grip.

"What we play or do not play, is completely dependent upon your behaviour," Penelope said. "Sit down as quickly as you can. I have had the most wonderful idea, and, am confident that even nanny, who is paid to do so, has not thought to play this game. It is an extra-special game, for an extra-special birthday girl," she said, smirking at Sophie.

"What is it? Please tell," Sophie said, clapping her hands and spinning round. "I told you my big sister, I mean my big step-sister, would join us. She is such good fun."

"Quiet! Be quiet and sit down and that includes you, Sophie," Penelope, said. "I suggest you lead your guests by example and if you all sit down, quietly, I will tell you the name of the game we are going to play."

Clarissa was peering through the window, searching through the fog for a glimpse of Penelope, when her legs buckled and she too became fixated with a scene from her own past. A scene she preferred to forget.

It had been a slow walk to the council offices, not least because Clarissa had dragged her feet every step of the

145

way. Darren let go of her hand as they approached the steps of the auspicious building.

"That's it," he said, as cheerily as he could. "I think it's best if you go in on your own, Claris. I will meet you in The Swan later and I'll have half a cider waiting for you. You can tell me what's been decided then. Everything crossed for good news. Go on, in you go."

"I don't want to go in there, Darren. Will you come in with me, please?"

"I can't do that, Claris. It's not a good idea. As much as I would like to, it's not the right thing, given the circumstances. If they see you have someone with you, supporting you, especially someone who has already got a roof over their head, they won't offer you anything. We have to play the game, unless you decide to go back home and bide your time a bit with your parents. Perhaps, in the circumstances, that would be the best solution for both of us. Everything has happened too fast, unplanned. It all feels a bit hasty. We haven't got a grip on it, on anything, to be honest. It might be a good idea to let the dust settle and go back to your parents for a bit. Put the brakes on our runaway car. Just for a few weeks, that's all."

"I've told you I am not going back there. It is not an option."

"Well, on those grounds alone, the council will have to sort something out for you, sharpish. Shall we make it seven o'clock in The Swan then? I'll be waiting for you in the snug and we can make a long-term plan then. A way forward, as they say. At least we will be together, Claris, I

146

can promise you that much. I am a man of my word, if nothing else," Darren, naively said.

Clarissa was denied a place on the emergency list on the basis that she already had an address, despite the fact that she refused to return to it, for personal reasons. Although sympathetic to her plight, the council officer encouraged her to return home in an attempt to iron out her differences with her parents, which, to all intents and purposes, seemed superficial and easily sorted. The officer had obviously heard similar stories on numerous occasions and, in the majority of cases, reconciliation was undoubtedly the best advice and preferred course of action. Downhearted, Clarissa was eventually referred to a charity shelter where she would be given a meal and a bed for the night. Hopefully this would provide her, and her parents, with a cooling-off period, if nothing else. Having secured her berth in the shelter she made her way to The Swan, if only for the comfort of its familiarity and in the hope that Darren would have devised a plan, even a temporary one.

Sitting on their table, in the corner of the snug, Clarissa watched the clock tick away the minutes until it reached and past seven o'clock. She fixed her gaze on the door, willing Darren to walk through it.

"Sorry, love," the bartender said, lifting her empty glass off the table, "but, I need to start clearing away. Have you been stood-up, by that young man of yours? There is no excuse for keeping a pretty, young lady waiting half the night. Mind you..."

"I am quite sure that I have not been stood up, as you so crudely put it. But, then again, you are probably like the

147

rest of the prejudgement pack who jump to the wrong conclusion, who put two and two together and come out with a hundred and four! Eager to see the worst in anyone who looks or sounds different."

"There is no need for that! I was only being polite and, I'll have you know that I hear all manner of things and see all types of people in here, and I've seen his sort before."

"His sort! What's that supposed to mean? Do enlighten me," Clarissa said, regaining a degree strength and a modicum of composure.

"If you must know, you are not the first young lady one of his kind has entertained in here and, no doubt, you will not be the last. I've heard them promising the world to girls like you to get what they want. He's a professional romancer, pie-in-the-sky bloke, if you ask me. Seen them all before."

"I am not asking for your opinion and how dare you accuse, condemn and pass judgement on someone you know nothing about. My boyfriend and I will be finding somewhere else to spend our time and money in the future. Somewhere half-decent, as well," Clarissa, said, standing up to leave.

"Good riddance, young lady, and good luck with that boyfriend of yours because you are going to need it. I can recognise his sort a mile off and it's nothing to do with the colour of his skin."

Clarissa wrapped her coat around her and instinctively made for Darren's home. She was sure she knew the street where he lived, if not the number of the house.

"It must be nippy out there," Josie, the receptionist said, walking over to shut the patio doors. "It's still quite foggy, a bit eerie, really. Reminds me of a smoke-filled arena, where no one can see a hand in front of their face but clearly hears the spinechilling shouts and taunts of spectators, echoing around it. I hope the sun breaks through soon. Fog clings to you." Josie shuddered, closing the door on Fred and Penelope. Little did she know that Fred was a gladiator, of sorts, in his own arena, fighting his giants of remorse.

CHAPTER
TWENTY-THREE

Fred was feeling more alive, having turned to face his fears, than he had ever done whilst running away from them. His mission to save Billy was fuelled by his determination to play the hero.

It is often said that one is given the strength from somewhere to refuel and fan dying embers. Fred was on fire. A fire ignited by his will to save his friend. Having cried out to a higher force and discovered the courage to beat his demons into submission, he was more than equipped to save his friend. Neither of the young soldiers would relinquish their oath of service, wherever their vow led them and whatever price they ultimately paid for it. The boys had done everything in tandem and realised that there are far worse things in life than dying in the service of their country, arm-in-arm.

How Fred managed to push the dilapidated wheelbarrow, with Billy slumped inside it, along the perimeter of the battlefield is anyone's guess. That he remembered silently begging for strength to do so, and the superhuman power which energised his muscles in response to his plea, challenged his scepticism of divinity. Faith, hope and love, despite the atrocities of war, were steadfast stabilisers in its uncertainties.

Finally, they reached the clearing in the wood where Fred had spent the previous night in the hollow of an oak tree, a hiding place, of sorts. It was as though the sounds of war were suspended, subdued and silenced again beneath the old oak's strong, steadfast branches.

"We'll rest here awhile, Billy. Get our breath back a bit," Fred said, "then we will make for the first aid post. They'll patch you up there and make you as good as new before you can say 'Jack Robinson'. Bet you'll be the first they've had brought in on a wheelbarrow, though!"

"Only you could have put me inside this thing and wheeled me out of there, Fred. Only you."

"Well, I couldn't have done it without Silver Mark2, could I, now?"

Billy, laughed, until the blood splurged through his parched, dry mouth.

"Stop laughing! It's not that funny," Fred said. "Mind, you, we didn't half have some fun growing up on the hill. No backsides in any of our trousers, but we didn't give two-hoots what we looked like. What fun we had. And, if nothing else, our upbringing taught us right from wrong, black from white, good from bad, didn't it? Now, stop laughing or you'll end up choking to death. I haven't pushed you this far to watch you pop your clogs perched on Silver Mark2," Fred, said.

"Stop making me laugh, then. It was great being in your gang, Fred. I would have followed my hero anywhere. Suppose we were blood brothers, of sorts, well we are

151

now," he said, gripping his stomach, in an attempt to stop the blood flow. "Do you think we'll make it, Fred? Go home together, I mean."

"Of course, we'll make it. We haven't come all the way from Goldendale to be laughed at and together we will make it home. Silver Mark2 will make sure we do," he said, tapping the side of the rusty wheelbarrow, caked in sludge.

"I'm not afraid to die, Fred, if we don't make it, I mean. It's a strange feeling. I thought I would be afraid of dying, but I'm not. Everything feels calm, peaceful and I've made my peace with my maker."

"That's enough of that talk. I've not pushed your backside half-way round the edge of a warzone, in a wheelbarrow, to have you die on me! Now, take a swig of this," he said, placing a bottle to his friend's lips.

"Where on earth did you get that from? It's a bit of good stuff. Nectar. I'm feeling better already," he spluttered.

"Ask no questions and you won't be told no lies, Billy. Only the best for you, lad, only the very best. Come on, let's make tracks. The first-aid post is that way, I think," he said, standing up and stretching his neck.

"Give us another five minutes, Fred. Just let me close my eyes. I've been wondering what this field looked like before the war. Before we landed on it. Expect it was full of flowers, daisies, buttercups, you name it, bet they all bloomed here. It must have been a great place for kids to play. Bet their fun and laughter filled the air, just like ours

152

did, but look at it now. Look what we've done to it. There has to be another way to settle disputes. A peaceful way. A way to iron out differences and right wrongs, without resorting to war, without killing our fellowmen."

"I'll say it again, that's enough of that kind of talk. There's no time to spare and you know what they say, 'there's no peace for the wicked', so we'd best get-going. The sooner I deliver you to the medics the sooner they'll sort you out. Bet there'll be a long line of pretty nurses waiting to get their hands on you, Billy. Let's go."

Although Sarah had stepped out of the discharge lounge, she could neither see nor hear Fred but had, however, come face-to-face with her own skeletons.

Having left her Mother sprucing herself up to meet with the group of merry windows, Sarah was gingerly making her way towards a private clinic and another appointment with destiny.

"Do take a seat. The specialist will be with you in a moment," a Personal Assistant, said. Sarah eyed her with cynicism. She could have completed every one of the secretary's duties with her hands tied behind her back and would probably have made a far better job of them than the woman sitting across from her, discretely filing her nails and flipping through the latest issue of 'Vogue'.

Life could have been so different had she accepted the position in London and how she wished she had done so, especially here, now, in this place. The intercom buzzed.

153

"The Doctor will see you now, Miss…let me see. Smith, that's right, Miss Smith. Through the double-doors, second door on the right."

"Thank you."

"Do take a seat, Miss Smith," the rather handsome, though slightly arrogant, specialist, said.

Sarah, who had donned her best outfit for the occasion, sat down. Another huge, mahogany desk, separated them. A desk not unlike every other barrier which had been used to separate the wheat from the chaff for the majority of her life. Desks in school classrooms, desks in waiting rooms and government offices, counters in banks and, of course, desks in all the corridors of power.

"Now then, let me see; here it is," he said, thumbing through a manilla folder. "I expect this news will come as no surprise to you. The test result is positive. You are in the family way, pregnant, my dear. Now, let us cut to the chase, shall we? How do you feel about the result, Miss? It is Miss, isn't it? Are congratulations or commiserations, the order of the day?"

"It is Miss and why shouldn't it be? I wonder, how you feel about that, Mister?" It is Mister, isn't it?"

The consultant smiled. "Touche, my dear. I take it that commiserations are, in this instance, the order of the day and that the pregnancy is unwanted, unplanned?"

Sarah stood up. "Unwanted, unplanned, unmarried, unemployed, unimportant, the list is endless. Yes, I am all

154

of those things and more, but I will not waste any more of your time or my money. Thank you for the results, doctor. The next few months will be rather busy, if not traumatic, ones."

The specialist made a half-hearted effort to leave the security, status and comfort of his highbacked chair, centrally placed behind his extra-large, solid wood, desk.

"Please do not attempt to make a courteous effort on my behalf. I know where the door is and I can show myself out. Good day, doctor."

"Well do not hesitate to contact my secretary if we can be of further assistance in what appears to be a delicate and somewhat difficult situation for you to juggle. It may be a comfort to realise that you are not the first to face the dilemma of an unwanted pregnancy and, I am equally confident, that you will not be the last young lady to walk through those doors in your condition."

Meanwhile, Penelope, accompanied by her own demons, was continuing to relive her step-sister's party. A day from which there would also be no escape nor diversion.

"We're all sitting down now, Penelope," Sophie said. "What game we are going to play. It's so exciting."

"First things first. It is a game which requires you to be as quiet as a nest of tiny mice. Do you think you can all do that, especially you, Sophie?"

155

"We can! Of course, we can," Sophie and her birthday playmates shouted.

"Very well. Huddle together, that's it. Now, place one of your fingers over your lips to remind you that you must not speak. When you are very quiet, I will explain the rules of the game. Listen carefully. The game we are about to play is called: 'Hide and Seek' and you all need to start thinking of a good place to hide. It should be a place where no one will ever be able to find you. Then, before anyone hides, I will close my eyes and count to one hundred. When you hear me shout, 'I'm coming ready or not!' you will know that I am looking for you. The last person I find will win the prize. Do you understand?"

"Yes, we do," Sophie and her playmates, shouted. "And what will the prize be? Please tell us," Sophie said.

"The prize will remain a secret until I discover who the winner is. There are lots of secret hiding places in the garden," she said, looking over the huge estate. "Do be quiet, children, or I will abandon the game before it has started. Fingers back on lips. The ten minutes of silent thinking, starts now."

Penelope smirked. Even nanny, with her many years of expertise, could not have closed the mouths of fifteen three-year olds, including her step-sister, so sublimely.

Clarissa was tentatively walking, carrying a heavy heart, along the front pavement of a row of terraced houses in the hope that Darren lived somewhere in the vicinity. Although it was getting dark, the street was a hive of activity. Doors

156

were constantly being slammed and raised voices bellowed obscenities through windows at boys playing football, in the middle of the road, under the street lights. Their efforts to score, between the items of clothing being used as goal posts, regularly sent the ball crashing into doors, windows and walls, resulting in a volley of abuse and verbal warnings from unfortunate residents. Outside one of the open doors an elderly man, sitting on a makeshift, old chair, was smoking a pipe and minding his own business.

"Excuse me, sir," Clarissa, said. "I wonder if you know where Darren Johnson lives? It's somewhere around here, in this street, I think."

"And, who wants to know?"

"My name is Clarissa, but that doesn't make any difference, does it? I'm a friend of his, that's all."

"Not a close enough friend to know where he lives. A true friend would know at least that much about him."

"I am his friend and he did tell me where he lives, but I've forgotten the number of his house. I'm sure it's in this street, though. Do you know him? I really need to see him."

The old man, sucked on his pipe, before spitting some of its black residue onto the floor. "I reckon you'll find him at number twelve, but you didn't hear that from me," he added, "assuming, of course, he wants to be found, especially by you."

"Thank you. I'm sure he will be pleased to see me."

157

"Don't be thanking me just yet. You'll have to get past his momma first and, take it from me, she's a force to be reckoned with. No one pulls the wool over her eyes, so tread careful, girl."

"I will," Clarissa said, striding more confidently down the street. "Number twenty, eighteen, sixteen, fourteen, twelve, this must be it," she said, gingerly lifting the brass knocker.

"Get the door, Darren, answer the bloody door, will you? Lord knows who's knocking at this time of night, but whoever it is tell them we've got no money and to come back tomorrow. I bet it's that rent man, again. He calls at all hours. Got the face of the devil, he has. Thinks we're made of money, so put him wise and tell him to swing his hook and send him packing," a woman, whom Clarissa assumed was Darren's mother, shouted.

Clarissa suddenly felt weak at the knees, faint. Darren had obviously told her the truth, at least about his home and had hinted that his mother was the boss of it. The house sounded overcrowded and, from what she could see and hear, it was a far cry from the home comforts she had taken for granted.

"Clarissa, what are you doing here? How on earth did you track me down?" Darren said, closing the front door behind him, afraid of being overheard.

"I waited in The Swan until the barman threatened to throw me out. Where were you? Why didn't you meet me? I couldn't wait in there, with no money and an empty glass, any longer."

"I can't talk to you here. My mother will have my guts for garters if she catches me. I haven't told my family about you yet and they won't be very happy when they find out. You've got to give me more time to break it to them, gently, get them used to the idea. Anyway, what are you doing here? What do you expect me to do at this time of night?"

"You promised you would meet me and I couldn't hang around in The Swan any longer. I had to come and find you because I thought there was something wrong. You would never deliberately stand me up, would you?"

"No, I wouldn't, but I couldn't get out. There's a lot going on here," he said, nodding towards the front door. "We are in debt up to our necks and I can't possibly tell them about you, not yet. It would sink the ship, then we would both be up to our necks in it. Anyway, I thought the council would find you somewhere to stay tonight."

"A shelter. A homeless shelter, Darren. Give it it's proper name. That's where I will be staying tonight."

"Well, it will only be for a few days at max. I'm sure the council will find you somewhere. Look, we will be together, but not just yet. Cut me a bit of slack."

"Who is it, Darren? Who are you talking to? I told you to send them packing, didn't I?" his mother called.

"You'll have to go now, Clarissa. I'll meet you at the hostel in the morning. I promise," he said, before closing and locking the door in her face.

159

"Looks like you've seen a ghost," the old man, sucking on his pipe, said. Clarissa gave him a wide berth and stared at the pavement beneath her feet. "Take it his momma sent you packing. She's good at doing that, if nothing else."

Fighting back tears, Clarissa didn't answer him and slowly made her way back to the night shelter. For the first time, since everything hit the fan, she momentarily considered returning home, but resisted the temptation, believing Darren would prove true to his word.

Back in the hospital's discharge lounge, Clarissa turned to Darren's baby boy, and whispered, "let's join the others outside for a breath of fresh air, shall we? A bit of fog never bothered me." Covering her baby's face with his blanket, she opened the doors and stepped outside, where she expected to find Fred, Sarah and Penelope.

"Have they finally been discharged, jumped ship, Josie?" Stan, cheerily asked, scanning the waiting area. "Another mission accomplished. Over and out!" he said.

"No such luck. They are all waiting outside, but I hope that's a step in the right direction and at least the fog seems to be lifting. Looks like we'll make our get-together later. Fingers crossed, hey."

CHAPTER TWENTY-FOUR

"Help! Someone, help us," Fred shouted, as he wheeled Billy through the tented entrance to the makeshift hospital.

The nurse, who ran towards them, took one look at Billy's wounds, and called for immediate assistance. "Surgical emergency," she shouted, pointing towards a bay on her righthand side.

"Careful with him," Fred said, to three orderlies, wearing white coats, stained with blood, as they started to transfer Billy onto a bed.

"Morphine," a doctor, said, jabbing a needle into Billy's side. "We'll get you patched up in no time," he assured him, although the look on his face belied his initial assessment.

Not many of the men, slumped on beds in the surgical bay, were calling out in distress or discomfort. Some were suffering the pain of their wounds, amputated limbs and all manner of surgical procedures, in silence. Despite every best effort to create and maintain a degree of morale, a heavy blanket of despair, inevitability, pervaded every corner of the portable hospital, seeping out from the wounded and dying. Members of staff did their utmost to portray a professional, controlled demeanour in the most appalling conditions. This was a very different battlefield, but a battlefield nonetheless, and, although he did not realise it, or admit to it, Fred was suffering from shellshock.

"You'll be as good as new, as right as rain, Billy. You mark my words. They'll sort you out in double-quick time. That's what they are good at," he told his playmate.

Reliving the situation as a spectator, Billy looked smaller than Fred remembered him. His ashen, dirty face and hands added to the stains on the once white, cotton sheets. The blood and sweat of previous patients had merged with his in the not-so-sterile environment where medics, whose artillery consisted of scalpels, lancets and morphine, wore very different uniforms.

"Fred, I'm honestly not afraid to die now. My father's bible came in handy, after all. At least, by God's grace, I have tried to do some good with the life I've been given. We both have, haven't we? It's important to leave the world a better place than we found it," he said, reaching for Fred's hand.

"We certainly have, Billy, but don't get giving the score at half time, the game isn't over yet. But, you are right, we have served our country and our fellowman as best we can. Come to think of it, some folk never learn to live before they kick the bucket, they just exist from one day to the next. We've had a good innings, if not a long one, Billy, and we haven't half enjoyed the ride. But hang in there, lad, we've still got everything to play for. Don't give up the ghost just yet."

Billy didn't answer, the morphine had started to do its job.

Sarah was slowly walking the distance between the private clinic and the place she called home. In truth, it was a home that would never belong to her, an elaborate sham, a roof and four walls owned and ruled by Mr William Davies. He owned every brick, every stick of furniture, including her. Yet, there was her mother, who had always featured in her decisions, to consider. "I will speak to William and tell him about the baby. His baby. Our baby. That is what I will do," she, whispered, turning the key, William's key, in the front door.

It was late in the evening when William arrived, typically unannounced. He'd had a demanding day, the effects of which, were etched into the deep furrows on his forehead. Sarah helped him to remove his coat and poured him a whiskey. He sank into his favourite armchair, put his feet up on a matching pouffe and stretched out in front of a roaring fire. As was her custom, Sarah sat on the floor, alongside him. He placed his hand on her long, dark, beautiful hair.

"This is sheer bliss, Sarah. You are my calm in life's storm, my oasis and haven." She sighed and turned to face him.

"There is something I would like to discuss with you."

"Not now, dear, especially if it concerns your mother. I do hope, however, that she is continuing to enjoy good health. She appears, of late, to be improving on every front."

"It is not about my mother, William," she said, repositioning herself on the edge of the pouffe and looking him straight in the eye.

"It's about me, us."

William started to run his finger around the edge of his whiskey glass, a habit he regularly resorted to whenever he felt uneasy, unsure. Sarah took it as a warning to change tack.

"It is nothing that will not wait, William, and nothing to concern yourself about. You look exhausted, my love. Try to relax. This is, after all, your private oasis, your calm in the storms of life. Let me top-up your glass."

"Very well, and then we will unwind together. Thank you, my love."

Penelope continued to watch Sophie's party game and although she tried to ignore the scene, she was mesmerized by the unfolding events of a day she had tried to erase from her memory.

"Gather round, children. That's it, squeeze in as close as you can. I want to tell you a secret. When I was a little girl, I found lots of nooks and crannies to hide where no one ever found me."

164

"Must we hide in the garden or can we go inside?" Sophie, asked.

"You must not go inside the house or you will be disqualified. Your hiding place must be somewhere outside."

"Where do you think is a good place to hide, Penelope?" Sophie whispered, tugging at her step-sister's dress.

"That is my secret and my hiding place. Now, kindly stop touching me and refrain from tugging at my dress."

"I think I know where it might be and I am going to find it and hide there," Sophie, said. Penelope ignored her.

"Quiet and listen carefully," Penelope, said. "I will go into the drawing room and start to count to one hundred, very slowly, while you all find somewhere to hide. Do you understand?"

"Yes," came the impatient, unanimous reply.

Clarissa had never felt so bereft and lonely. She tossed and turned through every minute of the night on an uncomfortable, bunk bed in a hostel for homeless women. Some of the older women, were battered and bruised in more ways than one, and cried themselves to sleep. She cupped her tummy, unable to believe that she was carrying a baby, Darren's baby, inside her. Surely he would be true to his word. He loved her, didn't he? He had obviously told her the truth about his family and their living conditions. There was, without doubt, no room for her in his overcrowded home and, from what she had seen and heard, she would never be invited to share it. But, if that was the case, what would become of them? She toyed, again, with the idea of returning home, if only for a short time, until Darren could provide for them, but she could not face the retribution and repercussions her condition would cause. The night in the hostel was a restless one, during which her limited options tumbled over and over in her young, naïve mind.

When morning came, as it always does, regardless of one's joys or sorrows, Clarissa was still without a clear solution to their situation. All she knew, without doubt, was that she loved Darren and was expecting his baby. Her parents, however, would never accept the truth of the matter. Their solution, she thought, would be to insist that the baby be put up for adoption to rid them all of an embarrassing problem. There was therefore no way back, no reverse gear. She had to step forward and learn to stand on her own two feet, even if that meant standing alone.

First in the queue at the council offices early the following morning, Clarissa's hope was revived, when Darren joined her on the steps outside the town hall's double doors.

"Thank goodness you are here, Darren. I need you," she said, linking him.

"I told you I would be here and I am. You can rely on me, one hundred percent. Please take me at my word, Claris," he said, holding her hand. "I'm sorry about last night. I had no alternative other than to play everything down to my mother, but let's do this together, shall we? I will sort my momma out later when I tell her about you and the baby. She'll come round without soap and water."

Fortune smiled on them, when the young woman manning the help desk, provided them with details of a small flat which had, only that morning, become vacant.

"This one has just become available," she said. "To be honest, there are others on the list who would snap it up in a flash, but your condition and situation has made you a priority and given you first refusal. May I suggest that you do not turn the offer down, though," she whispered, leaning towards them. "To do so, may jeopardise, even forfeit, your place on the list."

Clarissa's smile was wider than that painted across the face of any Cheshire cat. Darren clasped her trembling hand and said, "we have a home, Claris, we have a home to call our own".

"The fog is finally clearing," Josie, the receptionist said, peering out through the double doors, before tidying up the magazines and straightening the chairs. "Let's hope we don't get any eleventh-hour discharges now."

CHAPTER
TWENTY-FIVE

A doctor, wrapped in a blood-stained, once brilliant white, coat, asked Fred to join him at the entrance to the surgical bay.

"It is not, I am sorry to say, looking good for the young man you brought to us," he said, glancing towards Billy. "I am afraid gangrene is getting the better of him. It runs riot if wounds are left untreated. Had he arrived sooner, we may have been able to save him and, had it been confined to a limb, we may have been able to amputate. Sadly, this is one fight he is going to lose. As I say, gangrene is winning and we will do all we can to ease his pain and passing. I am sorry, awfully sorry, old chap," he said, patting Fred on the shoulder. "You made a valiant effort to get him here. We have never seen a wounded soldier wheeled in on a barrow before and probably never will again. You did all you could for him and that, given time, will be a comfort to you. I'll ask the padre to stop by when he gets a minute."

Fred hunched his shoulders, shrugging off the doctor's somewhat patronising, touch. It could not be true and, if it was, Billy would prove him wrong. He would be the first to fight extensive gangrene and live to tell the tale. He strode over and stood by the side of Billy's bed and whispered in his ear.

"Now you listen to me, Billy. You can stop playing dead and get your arse out of this bed. We've got another innings coming up and you're batting first." Billy didn't move a muscle or flutter an eyelid.

"Hello Billy, it is Billy, isn't it?" the padre, said, standing alongside Fred. "Don't be afraid, son. The Lord is with you," he said, touching Billy's hand.

"Don't be afraid!" Fred, said. "Why should he, of all people, be fearful? He is one of the bravest men I know and I can tell you now, in no uncertain terms, that he is going nowhere. I've made damn sure of that. He is staying here, with me. There's still plenty of work for him to do in this hellhole. Besides, he's too young to kick the bucket. Don't be afraid! That's a good 'un! Are you having a laugh, padre? I'll have you know that Billy has saved the lives of dozens of men and took a bullet for at least another two. Bet you've never had to stare down the barrel of a gun and give death a run for its money with your bible tucked under your arm, have you? You will never see or feel a fraction of what this brave, young man has done for his country. He never shrank back from the frontline, not once. What's more, padre, he's made his peace with God and he's afraid of nothing now, including the grim reaper."

The chaplain didn't flinch nor take offence. There was nothing, given the circumstances, he had not heard or seen before and one thing he had learned during his many years of service was to resist temptation in whatever guise it appeared. His battles were spiritual ones fought under a banner of love, forgiveness, mercy and eternal grace. Undeterred in his mission, he took Billy's hand in his own.

169

"There is no greater love than this, that a man lays down his life for his friends," he said. "Well done, thou good and faithful servant."

William, having left Sarah in the early hours of the morning was sitting at his breakfast table with his wife and children in a respectable, picture-perfect pose. His wife, oblivious to her husband's double-life and standards, felt secure in his love and provision for them. William perfectly balanced the façade he had created and never discussed his family life with Sarah for fear of diluting their comfortable, cosy, cohabitation with the fractured splinters of his façade.

"Sarah, I have something quite wonderful to tell you," her mother, sitting at their own breakfast table, said. Sensing her excitement, Sarah placed her teacup onto its saucer.

"And, what might that be, mum?" she said.

"It's a good job you are sitting down, Sarah and, it might be a good idea to put a tot of whiskey in that cup of tea. A rather nice gentleman, who belongs to our little circle of friends, has asked me to accompany him on a world cruise. We have been walking-out together for a few months but I never expected him to invite me, as his companion, on an all-paid, world cruise. I have barely slept a wink. I am so excited. Isn't it wonderful? You are pleased for me, aren't you? You look rather surprised."

"Surprised! I'm shocked to the core, mother. In fact, I am stuck for words." Her mother laughed and poured a double whiskey into her daughter's breakfast teacup.

170

"Well, we won't be sailing away for a couple of weeks, yet," she said. He is busy sorting tickets out, a suite with a private balcony, no less. It's an opportunity not to be missed, isn't it? A chance of a lifetime, especially at my age! Opportunity rarely knocks twice, so grasp it with both hands when it does! Well, that's my motto."

As much as she loved her mother, Sarah could not bring herself to comment and started to clear the breakfast table. All she could think about was every one of her own lost opportunities, especially the offer of working in London. She had let her own chance of a lifetime slip through her fingers and the predicament she was currently facing was another consequence of having made a wrong decision; an option taken in the interests of her mother's welfare.

"I am happy for you mum, truly I am, and you are right, opportunity rarely knocks twice in anyone's life. No one knows the truth of that more than I do and what's more, I am still living with the consequences of it."

"Quiet children," Penelope said. "Before you all run off to hide you must remember not to make a sound, because the last child I find will win today's extra-special, birthday prize."

"I think I know what the prize is and I am going to win it," Sophie said.

"I have told you that the prize is dependent upon who wins the game, birthday girl," Penelope, said. "To win the prize your hiding place must be an extra-special one, because I will endeavour to find you first. There will be no

171

concessions, step-sister. Now, off you go," she said, before turning her back on the children, randomly running around the garden, apart, that is, from Sophie, who knew exactly where she was going to hide; a place where no one, not even her step-sister, would find her.

"Time for a little snooze," Penelope said, stretching out on the chaise lounge. Absolute bliss. I do believe I am beginning to enjoy this little soiree."

After a timelapse of twenty minutes, or more, nanny appeared in the dining room.

"Where are the children, Penelope? Where's Sophie? What is happening and why are you lying down? I left you in charge of the children. Where, in God's name, are they all? I cannot even hear them."

"Calm down, nanny. Everything is under control, my control, and I have ensured that every one of the little cherubs has been completely and utterly occupied in your absence."

"Where are they? Answer me," nanny said.

"Careful, nanny. If you must know, they are playing 'Hide and Seek' and enjoying every minute of it, in absolute silence."

"Unsupervised! They are only three years of age."

"What harm could possibly befall them in the confines of the estate? I have played in the garden for hours and enjoyed every minute. It is simply fun and games. Do lighten up! Besides, it is obviously something that you have not thought to play with them, despite being paid to do so."

"Well, it's time we found them. All of them," nanny said, making for the patio doors.

Penelope pushed past her and shouted, "coming ready or not! That should do it, nanny. Let's start looking."

Clarissa's enthusiasm was quickly evaporating following the initial rush of excitement she had felt at the prospect of moving into a home of their own. Having signed all the documents associated with the rental, reality started to dawn. The flat was cold, damp and barren, a far cry from the home she had known and felt secure in. She realised that her parents would be upset if they could see where she was living although, even that, would not remove the ugly stain of prejudice and persecution from their hearts. Yet, she still longed to tell them, especially her mum, that she was expecting a baby, their first grandchild. But, the only benefit and comfort she possessed was in the knowledge that Darren loved her and wanted to share his life with her. The previous owners of the flat, who had done a midnight flit, had left some pieces of furniture, for want of a better word, behind them, including a bed-settee with fold down arms, and a well-worn armchair, of sorts. On a positive note, the tiny flat had plenty of hot, running water and an electricity supply. Being thankful for small mercies, given the circumstances, was, without doubt, their best policy. Clarissa's standard of living had dramatically changed and it would take time to adjust to it, but Darren was with her now and together they would create a peaceful palace from a hellish hovel.

"We'll soon get this place shipshape, Claris, especially before the baby arrives. A lick of paint will brighten it up no end and we can sleep on this settee until we get a proper bed. Charity shops will be our first port of call tomorrow. We'll pick up all we need from a tour of them at give-away prices. Come to think of it, I've heard there is a shop not far from here which helps to furnish homes for homeless folk, kit them out."

"Please stop referring to us as that, Darren. We are not homeless now, are we? We have a roof over our heads and I am grateful for that much. It is somewhere and something we will both have to adjust to. Mum used to call it cutting your garment to your cloth."

"It's only temporary, Claris. You wait and see. When I am king of the castle, you, my love, will be my queen," he said, placing his arms around her, and you, my baby boy, will be our prince."

"How do you know we are expecting a baby boy, Darren? Besides, it doesn't really matter what God gives us because our baby will be loved and that is the most important thing in life; to know that you are loved," she said, momentarily recalling the love and commitment her own parents had shown her.

"I've got a feeling he is a boy and we will call him Archie, after my grandfather, if that is acceptable to you, your majesty?" Darren, joked.

"It is more than acceptable, because, believe it or not, I had a granddad Archie, as well. Tell you what, you can choose a boy's name and I, your majesty, will choose a girl's.

"Deal," he said.

CHAPTER
TWENTY-SIX

"Would you allow me to pray with Billy?" the chaplain, asked, Fred. "It cannot do any harm and, who knows, it may help to improve his physical condition. Stranger things have happened in answer to prayer."

"Billy's not really a religious man. Well, not to my knowledge he isn't, but I don't suppose he would object to you saying a prayer for him in his hour of need. Thing is, he's been carrying his father's bible with him and I've spotted him reading it a couple of times. Then again, I should not have been surprised, he's a gentle soul. Wouldn't kill a fly when we were growing up and, at one point, I thought he was verging on pacifism, yet here he is, the bravest of our bunch."

"Extreme situations often unearth extreme courage. Fight or flight, that sort of thing," the chaplain, said. "I will say a short prayer with him and anoint him with a little holy oil, if that's ok?"

"I'll leave you to it then. I've got no heart nor head for prayers or talks of peace. My ears will be ringing with the sounds of war for the rest of my days."

"See you later, Billy," Fred said, before turning his back on his friend.

"The Lord is your shepherd, Billy," he overheard the padre say, as he headed towards the canvas doors and lit a cigarette.

"Did you mention that you had something you wanted to discuss with me, Sarah?" William said, stretching out in front of the fire. "I think it may have been something to do with your mother."

"Well, I do have something to tell you about my mother, William, something you may find hard to believe."

"Please don't tell me that she has taken a turn for the worse. She has been looking so much brighter recently, more alive."

"She is not ill, William. In fact, you are quite right about the change in her demeanour. She is far brighter. So bright that she's dazzled a gentleman friend into inviting her to join him on a world cruise!" William almost choked on his whiskey, before he spluttered and laughed out loud.

"Good for her. She's a dark horse, though," he managed to say between a bout of coughs and splutters.

Had Sarah not been worried about her own condition, she too, would have seen the funny side of the situation, but she had other, far more important, things on her mind.

"Don't you find it the least bit amusing, Sarah? We didn't see it coming, did we? Little wonder she's got a sparkle in her eye and a spring in her step. World cruise!" he said, holding his back and laughing out loud. "Well, at

177

least it means that we will be alone, just the two of us, nice and cosy, the way I like it."

"It is about that concept that I would like to speak to you, William."

"About what? The concept of being alone together, nice and cosy." Sarah shuddered.

"How would you feel about not being entirely alone with me? About sharing me with someone else, I mean."

"What on earth are you talking about? You don't have a sister or brother or some waif and stray waiting to join us as soon as your mother sails off into the sunset, do you? We are not a charitable institution, my dear."

"I have no siblings and it is not a waif or stray, it is just a baby, our baby. I'm expecting your child," she said, with her back turned to him.

"That's it, nanny. All present and correct," Penelope, said, counting the heads of fourteen excited children who had shown no ingenuity whatsoever in choosing a hiding place."

"But, where's Sophie. I cannot see her. Stand still, all of you, just for a minute," nanny, said. "She's not here, Penelope. Sophie isn't here. Where is she?"

"I'll find her for you, nanny. There is no need to panic. Your birthday girl is probably assuming that she has won the prize, but little does she know that the maker of the rules holds the right to change them at the drop of a hat. I do hope she is not too disappointed when she realises that there is never a prize for coming last in anything. That, nanny, is my birthday treat for her and the sooner she learns the truth of that fact, the better it will be for all of us. Leave it to me, nanny. I'll find her.

"Sophie, come out, come out, wherever you are. The game is over and I am coming to find you, ready or not!" Penelope called, striding across the lawn.

"Let's go indoors, children," nanny, said. "Sophie will be with us presently. Penelope knows every hiding place in the garden and will soon find Sophie. Let's put her birthday cake in the middle of the table, and when she joins us you can all shout, 'Happy Birthday' before she makes her wish. I'm sure you will enjoy doing that," nanny said, ushering the children into the dining room.

"Come out, come out, wherever you are! The game is over, Sophie," Penelope shouted, on her way past the huge, tiered fountain, the centrepiece of her poppa's estate. "Silly, stupid, Sophie, where on earth is she? One has far better things to do than waste time searching for a puerile step-sister."

Clarissa and Darren made an admirable job of kitting out their flat on a shoestring. It felt instantly warmer but was a far cry from becoming a home.

"I'll be back before you know it, Claris. I just need to let my momma see my face. She will never rest unless she sees me with her own pair of eyes. I promised her that I would let her know where I was, keep her in the picture. I'll be back before you have had time to miss me, so no worries," Darren said.

"Do you have to go? Please stay."

"Now, now," he said," kissing her on the cheek. "I've told you that I'll be back before you have had time to turn around," he said, closing the door behind him and flying down the tenement's fire escape.

As much as she loved and trusted Darren, Clarissa felt uneasy, restless and walked over every inch of the flat in an attempt to calm her fears. She stood over a Moses basket they had bought from one of the charity shops, tracing her fingertips along its wicker weave, unable to believe that she would be placing a baby, her baby, inside it in less than six months' time. Her heart became heavy. She missed her parents, especially her mum, and the security of their home comforts. Overcome with fatigue and foreboding, she nestled into an armchair in the sparse living room and fell asleep.

It was cold and dark when Clarissa woke. The room was as empty and as lifeless as the crib in its corner. Still half asleep, all manner of scenarios swamped her. What if Darren had deserted her? Left her bereft, with no one to turn to, to love and care for her and their baby. She covered herself with a blanket, curled up and went back to sleep, hoping that Darren would wake her from her dreams and all would be well.

CHAPTER TWENTY-SEVEN

"See you later, Billy" were the last words, apart from the Pardre's prayers that Billy heard before he left this world. But the words which would haunt Fred for the remainder of his life were the ones spoken by the doctor after his assessment of Billy's injuries.

'I am afraid gangrene is getting the better of him. It runs riot if wounds are left untreated. Had he arrived sooner we may have been able to save him and, had it been confined to a limb, we may have been able to amputate. Sadly, this is one fight he is going to lose. As I say, gangrene is winning and we will do all we can to ease his pain and passing. I am sorry, awfully sorry, old chap.'

If only Fred had managed to get Billy to the medical post sooner, if only he had not deserted him, left him for dead on the battlefield and wasted an entire night hiding in a tree like the coward he was, then perhaps the outcome would have been different and his friend would not have died. If only.

"It is my fault that Billy died that day. He always followed my lead. He trusted me with his life and I let him down," he said, and that was, in part, true.

"A baby, Sarah!" William said. "Surely not!"

"I am quite sure, William. There is no doubt whatsoever about my condition. I, we, are expecting a child," she said, kneeling down on the floor, alongside him.

William stood, bolt upright, onto his feet and brushed her aside, firmly placing his whiskey glass on top of the mantlepiece. Despite the raging fire, the room felt strangely cold. He turned to face her, a look of disdain shrouding his features.

"Then, you are in breach of the terms of our contract, my dear. The clause in question clearly states that you will take the necessary steps to ensure that you never, under any circumstances, become pregnant. You are aware of that clause, are you not, and, its consequences if breached?"

"I am, William, and please believe me when I tell you that I have taken every possible step to prevent this pregnancy but, nevertheless, I am expecting a child, our child. I am sorry," she said, standing to her feet, to join him. "I will, of course, ensure that the child does not affect our arrangement and that it will never become an inconvenience or an additional expense, to you and our relationship."

"You are absolutely right on both counts, Sarah. As you are fully aware, I already have a family and I will never allow you or your child to overshadow or impinge on that. Unfortunately, you are in breach of our contract and have until the end of the month to make alternative arrangements."

"But… but…"

"There are no buts, my dear. You have until the end of the month to find somewhere to live, unless, of course, you decide to uphold the terms of our agreement by making your little mistake disappear. In which case, life will resume, as normal."

"Would you honestly leave me little choice in this vitally important matter, William? Let us not be hasty, my love," Sarah said.

"My mind is set and the terms of our agreement must be upheld and fulfilled or forfeited. The choice is yours."

"A Hobson's choice is giving me no choice whatsoever. I have no option, given your stance, other than to comply with your terms, against my natural desire and better judgement. You have my word that I will endeavour to fulfil every clause in our agreement."

"That's my girl," he said, placing his arm around her. "Now then, let us not mention this little mishap again. I will put your discretion behind us, draw a line underneath it and, in so doing, normal service will resume immediately. Please pour me another," he said, passing her his whiskey glass.

"God help me! I have missed every one of life's opportunities and ended up here, in this condition," she whispered, obediently filling his glass. Her perfunctory duties had resumed but, although she was not yet conscious of it, her heart had fractured from the force of William's blow. Not all beatings are physical and not all bruises and wounds are visible. The deepest and most painful ones are those borne in silence and unseen by the naked eye.

Penelope had searched as many of the garden's hiding places that she could remember and meandered towards its outbuildings.

"There you are," Penelope said, picking up Sophie's birthday tiara off the floor, as she walked towards the last stall in the block of stables.

"I should have known that you would be hiding in here! Come out, you little nuisance. The game is up and there is no prize to be claimed. You have lost the game. Show yourself, now!"

But Sophie did not appear and Champion, with fear-filled eyes, reared up on his strong, hind legs, as his mistress, approached him.

"There, there, Champion, my beauty," she said, reaching for his reins. "Quiet now. I'm here. There is nothing to fear." But, there was a lot to fear, for at that very moment, Penelope saw her step-sister's crumpled body beneath Champion's feet.

"What have you done you silly girl?" she shouted, at Sophie's, motionless body. "Calm down, Champion. I'm here now," she reassured him, grabbing his reins and stroking his mane, before leading him outside.

"Sophie's here," she shouted, across the estate. "I have found her hiding in the stables. She has had an accident, an unfortunate accident." Tragically, the little birthday girl was beyond all earthly help. Champion had trampled her to death.

Just before the sun started to set over Lord Cuthbertson's estate, long after Sophie's birthday guests had left, and the doctor had sedated her parents, nanny started to clear the dining room table.

"She never got to blow out her birthday candles and make a wish," nanny, said, turning to face Penelope. "And, I think we both know what that wish would have been for, don't we? But, you were too mean-hearted to grant it. Had you done so, our princess would be here now.

"How dare you speak out of turn, nanny? Penelope said. "Kindly keep your misplaced assumptions to yourself. Sophie was a silly girl. A silly, stupid, girl who will not be missed."

"I will not keep silent. Had you granted her wish, Sophie would still be here now. Your selfishness and hatred resulted in her death and the truth of that fact should be recorded on her death certificate and etched on her epitaph."

"How dare you! Your days are numbered here, nanny. I will make sure they are."

Sophie's crumpled, broken body was eventually taken from the stately home by the local undertakers. Heart-wrenching screams, despite the administration of sedatives, echoed across the estate into the early hours of the morning. The inquest into her death concluded that she had attempted to ride the steed whilst it was stabled and he had thrown her to the ground and trampled her underfoot. Accidental death was the coroner's verdict but there was little doubt in anyone's mind who had been complicit in the accident and Sophie's demise.

Clarissa opened her eyes in the early hours of the morning in response to someone banging loudly on the front door. Darren must have forgotten his key.

"I'm coming," she called, reaching for the door handle.

"Out of my way," a boisterous woman, said, barging past her. "I suggest you sit down. Clarissa, isn't it? I am here to tell you a few home truths about my Darren. Make yourself comfortable, this won't take long."

"Who are you and where's Darren? He's not ill, is he?"

"He is not ill, in fact, he has never felt better. I am Darren's mother and am here to inform you that you will not be seeing my son again. I have other plans for him. Plans which do not include you or your baby. I understand that you are expecting a baby, is that true?"

"I am and it is Darren's baby. Our baby," Clarissa said, slumping into the tattered armchair.

"That may well be true, but Darren is already spoken for. In fact, he is engaged. I expect he did not tell you that, did he?"

"He told me that you had someone in mind for him," Clarissa managed to stutter.

"That is so typical of Darren. He can be very conservative with the truth when it suits his cause. They are childhood sweethearts who have been pledged to each other for many years. They share common interests and purpose."

"But he loves me."

"No, he does not love you. He is engaged, betrothed, to another and I suggest that you return home, to your parents, your own sort. You are not welcome in our family circle just as he is not acceptable to yours.

"But what about the baby?"

"Only time will tell if there is a baby or if it has all been a figment of your imagination, a ploy to tie my Darren down. The sooner you return to your parents, the better. Never attempt to contact my son again. His fling with you is over, he has sown his wild oats and he will be settling down soon," she said, making for the door. "You will not see him again."

Clarissa could not move. She had been hit by a ten-ton weight. Bowled over and almost out.

"Whatever will become of me, of us, now? It cannot be true. Darren loves me. I know he does," Clarissa said, caressing her tiny bump and lovingly eyeing the empty cradle in the corner of the sparse, living room.

"Have they all finally been discharged?" Stan, said, walking towards the reception desk.

"Not yet. They are all still outside in the garden, but their transport is on its way. I'm just hoping we have seen the last of the fog, though. I'm more than ready for our debrief. Our vocations can be a bit depressing if we take everything we see and hear to heart, can't they? Life doesn't seem fair, does it?"

"You are right about that; it's been an odd shift. Can't put my finger on it really. There has been quite a lot of new admissions though so it will be good to see some of them discharged. At least the fog has started to lift, although it's still a bit patchy here and there. Tell you what, I'll pop back in an hour or so. I am pretty sure it will have cleared by then and everything will be more or less back to normal."

"I'm sure it will," Josie, said, "and I'm pleased the sunlight is doing its best to break through, it brightens everything up."

CHAPTER
TWENTY-EIGHT

"I'm sorry Billy," Fred said, holding his head in his hands, sitting on a garden bench, in a quiet corner of the hospital grounds.

"You trusted me and I let you down, deserted you when you needed me the most. Left you for dead, I did. I'm not your hero, I'm no one's hero. Truth is, when push came to shove, I was a coward. When I was a lad, I used to imagine that making my coat into a cape and hanging it round my neck, made me invincible. Boyhood bravado, that's all it was, with no substance whatsoever. At one point, I honestly thought I had been born to save the world and truth was, I couldn't even save you, my brother in arms. Left you for dead in a field. And, if that wasn't condemnation enough, they went and pinned a medal on my chest for bravery. Did you know that? A medal for courageously wheeling you into the military hospital on a wheelbarrow and, even worse, your mother thanked me for doing my best to save you. You will never guess what my response to that was, Billy? I only went and told her that you died a hero without feeling a thing!"

Fred paused, uncomfortable with his confession. He looked down, examining his hands.

"You paid the ultimate price in the line of duty to save the lives of others in a service you didn't really believe in, but revered, nonetheless. To add insult to injury, they went and sent your mother one of those 'sorry for your loss letters', typed by some unknown stenographer, in the hope of nullifying the pain of your loss. My part in it all was pathetic. I may as well have stuck the bayonet into you myself, twisted it round, and left you to die on your own. I even walked away from your hospital bed and chickened out of saying goodbye to you. I felt nothing, Billy, nothing at all. You see, you weren't the only one who died in that makeshift hospital that day, because you took the best part of me with you. You will never know how many times I have prayed for a second chance, a second innings on the playing field alongside you, a chance to set the record straight, another chance to save you. I don't know how I managed to stand to attention at your funeral but I did my duty and played my part to perfection. Two of the soldiers, whose lives you saved, stood on either side of me. They took great pride, and a degree of comfort, from telling me and your family that they owed their lives, their futures and any family they would be fortunate to have, to your bravery."

"I'm so sorry, Billy," Fred said, falling to his knees and trembling from the top of his head to the tip of his toes.

At that moment, a ray of sunlight penetrated the fog and from nowhere, Billy stood in front of him.

Sarah, despite her promise to William, could not find it in her heart to rid herself of their little mishap and hoped, given time, William would relent and accept the situation. She should have known better. William already had a family, a life he prized above all else, a respectable façade he would never risk infecting. Sarah was his mistress, nothing more, and although she desperately tried to persuade him of the situation, he did not relent. Everything soured, and the sweetness of their relationship became rancid, toxic.

Initially agreeing to William's terms and conditions, over lunch in an upmarket restaurant, was not the first time Sarah had used the needs of her mother to camouflage her own insecurities. During counselling sessions, to which Sarah was referred, she realised that she had used her mother as an excuse to decline life's opportunities. Her mother was, in fact, Sarah's hiding place from fear. Fear that she did not possess the grounding, etiquette and confidence to hold her head high and walk through London's halls of fame. Fear of those who sat on high-backed, leather chairs, behind solid wooden desks and intimidated her. Her reluctance to grasp all of life's opportunities had little to do with her mother's needs, but rather her own insurmountable, mountain of self-doubt and fear. A lack of higher education, decorum, appropriate clothing and social standing were a few of the many hurdles she had fallen at. Invariably, she thought of herself as a social outsider, rather like a cuckoo in an uncomfortable nest, a situation and status she succumbed to and allowed to confine her, using her mother as an excuse to hide behind.

As soon as Sarah's pregnancy became obvious, William tightened the legal screw and severed his relationship with her. Returning to the tenement block, which she detested, she hit rock bottom.

Reflecting on her life, in the hospital's garden, she realised that her fears had invariably dominated her decisions and, when the chips were down, she could not blame anyone other than herself for every one of her shortcomings. Her biggest sorrow, however, was the loss of her stillborn baby. In the darkest, loneliest night, she often thought she heard him cry, longing to be loved. Throughout her pregnancy, in a deprived state of destitution, she neglected herself and wished her baby away too many times to number. He obviously heard her plea and was stillborn.

"I am sorry, little one," she whispered, sitting on the opposite end of the endless garden bench, "if I had my time again, I would fight for you with every fibre of my being. I would tell you, above everything and anything else, that you were loved, wanted and cherished. It is surely the things that money cannot buy which, at the end of the day, are life's most precious treasures. Please forgive me."

In response to her cry a shaft of light appeared in the corner of the garden, illuminating a crib. Sarah timidly made her way towards it.

Penelope never shed a tear and demonstrated no hint of remorse for Sophie's death. If anything, her heart became harder, stone-cold and her stiff upper-lip, strengthened. In truth, she was delighted that she no longer had to share her poppa with Sophie and truly believed that everything would revert to normal, to the life she had adored, before her step-family arrived in her utopia. How naïve of her to imagine that life would ever be the same following the loss of a child. Every inch of the huge estate was empty without

Sophie's light to brighten it. Poppa missed her more than words could say, a fact which Penelope detested, but the worst of the incident's repercussions were about to befall her.

"Miss Penelope, your poppa is waiting for you in the drawing room," nanny, said. "Please stop whatever you are doing and kindly join him, that's a good girl."

"Do I have to, nanny? And, kindly do me the courtesy of not referring to me as a girl! I am almost a teenager and, as such, I am extremely busy planning my birthday party. I feel inclined to invite every one of my friends, although I was tempted to exclude a few of them, just to see their disappointment, but have decided against it. Everyone will be so envious of me."

"Yes, your poppa wants to see you now, immediately. Hurry along. You can finish your invitations later."

"Very well. I expect he has something rather nice to tell me or to give me. It has been so very boring lately, but my party will cheer everyone and everything up. You'll see nanny. It will be such fun."

"Hello, poppa," Penelope said, sidling over to him and linking her arm beneath his. He immediately stopped leafing through his paperwork and placed his halfmoon glasses on the bureau.

"Let us take a seat, over there, shall we?" he said.

"Not on the chaise lounge, poppa. Let us sit on the love seat. That's it. I can see you now," she said, tucking her feet underneath her.

Her father looked weary, sad. Not least because his wife, after Sophie's funeral, had taken to her bed and had rarely been dressed or seen in public since. The house was a miserable place. There was a heaviness in the air, which was seeping into her father's features, slowly devouring his character. There was nothing fun-loving and light-hearted about him, anymore.

"What is it, poppa? You look so sad," Penelope said. "I know, we must do something to cheer us all up. It is so dreadfully quiet in here, rather like a mausoleum, I think that is what one calls it. I know, shall we plan my birthday party together? I am in the process of sending out my invitations. Wait until everyone knows that there will be a circus, acrobats, a big top and a huge funfair on the lawn. I am so terribly excited. Every one of my guests will turn green. What fun we will have," she said, clasping her hands. Her father sighed.

"It is about your birthday party, princess, that I have asked to see you. I need you to respond as a grown-up to what I am about to tell you. Can you do that for me?

"Of course, I can. I am grown up, poppa. I am almost thirteen now."

"Very well. Your step-mother and I, have been extremely sad since Sophie left us so tragically. Her loss is particularly difficult for my dear wife, your step-mummy, to accept," he said, and paused. For once, Penelope, remained silent, sensing a sombre seriousness, surrounding him.

"There are three very important things I have to tell you Penelope and, I hasten to add, I take no pleasure whatsoever in what I am about to say. Furthermore, it is highly likely that you will feel a degree of disappointment, but I trust you will respond to the situation in a manner that becomes your status. A stiff upper lip, and all that."

"What is it, poppa?" she said, gripping her legs more tightly.

"Firstly, your birthday celebration will be a much quieter affair than previously planned. It is inappropriate to celebrate so soon after Sophie's death…"

"But… but…" Penelope, said.

"Please do not interrupt me again," he said, raising his hand, but avoiding eye contact.

"The decisions we have made are not open for discussion and have been taken in the light of our huge loss. The second decision concerns Champion. I am very sorry to inform you that your steed has been sold and will be transported from the estate within the next few days. We are fortunate that someone has agreed to take him, ungelded as he is, despite the fatal incident. Lastly, my princess, I have acted on your complaints about nanny and am pleased to tell you that her services will no longer be required since you will be leaving us to attend boarding school in London, from the beginning of September. I am confident that this will prove to be your opportunity of a lifetime and one which will enable you to put Sophie's loss behind you, whilst affording you the very best education and prospects."

Penelope screamed so loudly and for so long that nanny burst into the room.

"There, there!" she said. "Whatever is going on? What on earth is all the fuss about?"

"Don't you dare touch me," Penelope cried, as nanny approached her. "None of you touch me, including you poppa. I hate you. I hate you all," she sobbed. "And, I hate her, I hate Sophie. I will always hate her. This is all her fault."

Standing on the sidelines and watching the replay of that fateful day all over again, Penelope, relived the impact of the life-changing consequences imposed on her. It was, by her reckoning, the very worst of days. Sophie, in life and death, had ruined everything. For her part, Penelope refused to feel the slightest twinge of remorse or regret and certainly felt no sorrow for the death of her step-sister and the termination of nanny's contract. Finally, she managed to close her eyes. She had seen enough. But, what she never expected to see, when she opened her eyes again, was Sophie, as clear as day, standing in front of her, reaching out her tiny hand towards her.

"You are just a figment of my imagination," she said, "that is all you are."

Clarissa, still reeling from the shock of Darren's mother's impromptu visit, had come to the conclusion that she had lied to her. His mother must have lied because Clarissa knew, without doubt, that Darren loved her. He had given her his word and she trusted him. But, what if it was true? What if Darren did not love her and she was all alone and expecting a baby, his baby? Thankfully, she still possessed enough common sense to realise that she needed a back-up plan. There was only one thing for it. She closed the door behind her and made her way to the red telephone box, on the High Street, outside The Swan, and inserted her last tuppence, the cost for a few minutes, into the black box. With a trembling finger she dialled her home telephone number, before hovering over Button 'B' preparing to retrieve her last tuppence if no one answered the phone.

"Hello," a man's voice, said. 'Beep... beep... beep' the black box demanded payment if she wanted to be connected. She pressed button 'A'. There was no going back now and there was no point in pressing button 'B' to get her money back.

"Is that you, Dad? Is Mum there? I need to speak to her. Please put her on. It's Clarissa and I haven't got any more change for the phone box so please put mum on."

"I know who it is and you will have a hard job to speak to your mother. She's in hospital. That's where your mother is."

"She can't be, dad. Mum's never ill. What's the matter with her? Tell me."

197

"Well, you should know the answer to that question, Clarissa. There is no doubt in my mind, why she's is in hospital, it's because you've put her in there."

"Don't be silly. I've done nothing wrong. It's you who is the bigot in all of this. Now, when and where can I see mum? I need to see her as soon as possible. It's urgent."

"Not likely, over my dead body! It's your fault that your mother is in there and the best thing you can do now is to make the most of a bad job and keep your distance from both of us. You have made your bed and, by God, you will have to lie on it. There is no coming back. I only hope your mother recovers because if she doesn't… well, let's hope she does, for your sake," he said, slamming the receiver down and cutting her off.

Clarissa watched the replay with tears streaming down her face. Clutching Archie to her heart and momentarily touching the letter her father had written to her, informing her that her mother had died, she slumped onto the bench in the hospital garden.

"I'm sorry, mum," she whispered, and, as she looked up her mother, who was only a few steps in front of her, smiled.

CHAPTER TWENTY-NINE

Fred, Penelope, Sarah and Clarissa had all, in very different ways, relived their regrets, but there was more to see and hear if they wanted to silence the echoes of the past, forever.

"This may come as a surprise to you, Fred," Billy said, "but, no one is perfect, not even you. We are human, prone to wander and fail. We each have our share of fears to conquer, so, do me a favour, and stop beating yourself up about yours. You did the best you could in the living hell we faced. War changes people. Brings out the best and worst in all of us."

"Well, it definitely brought the best out in you, Billy, but not so in me. I failed you, my regiment, my country and my honour and, guess what, they went and stuck a medal on me for doing it! Got away with murder, I did."

Billy sat down, alongside his friend, on the garden bench.

"The most courageous thing we can do, Fred, is to admit our weaknesses and shortcomings. Hold up our hands, with the rest of mankind, and admit the truth. We are all imperfect, yet we stand together, flawed as we are, against evil. We stand, having done all, to be counted for who and what we believe in, which sustains and strengthens us in times of need and will never leave or forsake us.

One of the many things I felt when I was dying on the battlefield, Fred, was not anger or bitterness, but mercy and compassion for those around me, including you, especially you. I have no idea where those feelings came from at the eleventh-hour of my life, but I am grateful for them."

"It is too late for me, Billy. You are flogging a dead horse, mate."

"It is never too late, for any of us, Fred and that is what I am here to tell you."

I am not worth it, Billy, and am sorry that it has taken me so long to admit it. I would give my life for you, here and now, without flinching. I remember the army padre saying, 'that there is no greater love than this, that a man lays down his life for his friends'. Thank you for giving your life for me, Billy, and for those who stood alongside me at your funeral. Edward Smithson, an officer and a gentleman, and Archibald Noble, a young private, who both owed their lives and futures to your bravery. Indebted to you, they are, and always will be."

Sarah timidly approached the wooden crib, overflowing with straw, in a quiet corner of the garden. Her steps were unsure, unsteady and full of trepidation, but she need not have feared. Tears streamed down her face and her heart overflowed with love, as she reached into the crib and touched the baby boy's, face.

"I am the father of the fatherless," a voice, said, "and this child's name was engraved on the palm of my hand from time immemorial."

"I am sorry, so very sorry," Sarah, said, reaching into the crib. "Can you forgive me for not wanting you, not loving and cherishing you, my beautiful, baby boy?"

"You were not to blame for the loss of this little one," a voice, that sounded like ripples of clear, pure water, said. "Whilst it is true that you erred in your judgement and were misled by your fears, it is not one's mistakes that define a soul, but rather the courage to own them and seek forgiveness. No one gives the score before the game is over, and I have not called time yet."

At the same moment, Penelope turned to face Sophie.

"Hello Penelope," I am so happy to see you," the child, with ringlets in her hair, said. "I have really missed you."

"Well, I have not missed you, phantom or not. You are the very last person I would engage in any form of conversation with. I have banished every thought of you from every moment of my life. Wiped you off my slate of remembrance. You are purely a figment of one's imagination, a reaction to medication or dehydration, nothing more."

"But, I longed to see you, Penelope, because I wanted to tell you that I am sorry and ask you to forgive me," she said, stretching out her tiny hand towards her, again.

201

"What on earth are you talking about? Forgive you! Whatever for, you silly girl?"

"For ruining your life. I did ruin it, didn't I? But, I did not mean to spoil everything for you and I am sorry."

"I cannot believe I am conversing with an illusion which is obviously due to tiredness, nothing more. And yet, I am prepared to indulge you, simply because you have rightfully acknowledged your place in my life. At least, spectre or not, you have admitted the truth. You destroyed my world and are the last person I would ever want to see."

"But why didn't you like me, Penelope? I loved you. I still love you."

"That's enough of that talk. Sentimental drivel."

"I am sorry for hiding in the stables on my birthday. I wanted to surprise you and I thought that riding Champion would be my prize for winning the game."

"Surprise me! Your puerility cost me everything I prized, everything I loved. Life was never the same after that prank. I was sent away to boarding school, the cruellest form of punishment imaginable. It was purgatory. Everyone hated me. I had no friends, no family and no one to turn to. My life was utterly miserable, and all because of you. You ruined my life."

"I am sorry, Penelope. I did not mean to hurt you. I loved you. Please forgive me."

"Oh! Do be quiet, Sophie."

"I will only be quiet if you forgive me. Please say you will."

Faced with a plea to forgive the child, the very one Penelope had wronged, the block of ice inside her heart involuntarily began to melt and the scales, veiling her selfish eyes, dissolved. For the first time, Penelope saw Sophie as the innocent child, she was and had always been and, in that split-second, she saw her own, ugly, warped, heart, tightly wrapped in barbed-wire. Gaining a degree of composure, she chose to brush the fleeting awareness aside, conscious that she still held sway over the child; the power to forgive or condemn. The choice, the final choice, was hers and hers alone. Unwittingly, Penelope placed her case, her stance, onto the scales of justice. It was true, Sophie had indeed ruined her life and surely someone, somewhere, should pay the price for having committed the crime. Justice demanded an eye for an eye, vengeance. Having had her eyes opened by a glimmer of truth, Penelope sensed the sword of Damocles hanging from the finest of hairs over the top of her own head. Perhaps it was her fear of the weakness of the thread, precariously holding the sword in place, that enabled her, given her own condemnation, to place mercy on the opposite side of the scales, in the hope of counterbalancing justice. Penelope was indeed the guilty one and although she had pointed the finger of blame at another, the child before her was innocent and continued to love her, despite everything. Before Penelope could pronounce judgement, Sophie, tugged at her dress.

"I love you, Penelope, I have always loved you. Please forgive me."

"There is nothing to forgive, Sophie. It was not your fault, I was to blame, not you. I am the guilty one," she said, wiping away an ice-cold tear.

"Then shall we forgive each other?" Sophie said, shielding her eyes from the sun's rays.

Clarissa, cradling Archie, stepped towards her mother.

"I am so pleased to see you, Mum. Look who I've brought to meet you. This is Archie, your grandson."

Clarissa's mother pulled back the shawl to reveal her grandson's tiny face. "He is beautiful, just like you," she said, "and Archibald is a good name."

"I have named him after granddad. It's a good, strong name, isn't it? And, I have told him everything I can remember about his namesake."

"Your grandfather was a brave man, who stood his ground on the battlefields of life more than once for those he loved. Defended us to the hilt, he did, and he would do it all again in a heartbeat, if he had to. He was straightlaced and called a spade a spade, though. Everyone knew exactly where they stood with your grandad Archie."

"Did you hear that, Archie? You've got a lot to live up to, my boy."

"Mum, I wanted to tell you that I am thinking of going back to college. I am determined now to reach for my stars and grasp them, if only for Archie's sake. He needs to know that nothing is impossible or beyond his reach. Life will be harder for him with more than his share of mountains to climb. Prejudice, in all its forms, is cruel."

"I am still of the opinion that qualifications are important, Clarissa, but you were right, about love, I mean," her mother said. "We cannot take qualifications with us when we leave this world, but there is no limit on the amount of love we can carry with us. In fact, it is the only collateral of any value. I am so sorry that I rejected Darren and missed my opportunity to get to know him. I should not have done and, if I had my time over again, I would shake his hand and welcome him into our family. I was wrong."

"I am sorry too, mum. Life seems pointless without you to share it with, and yet, I know that somewhere you will always be cheering me on and fighting my corner, you always have and, no doubt, you always will."

CHAPTER
THIRTY

"They've all finally been discharged then?" Stan said, peering round the hospital door. "The car park hasn't half been busy with pick-ups. They've been queuing outside to get in."

"Yes, they have all gone home, thank goodness, and I'm making the most of the lull, while it lasts," Josie, said. "Just hope there's no last-minute discharges in the pipeline. Nothing on the system, though, so that's a good sign. Must say, it's so much brighter out there now that the sun has finally broken through. That fog was an absolute pea-souper. I thought it was never going to lift. What a day! Little wonder, I'm as dry as a bone."

"If there's nothing spoiling, would you like to pop out for a quick coffee, then? We could get one out of the machine in the common room."

"Don't know if I dare. We never clock-off in this job, do we? Then again, everything is sorted and there isn't anyone waiting," she said, glancing at the clock.

"Let's nip out for a brew then. Come on," Stan, said. "It's been a long and difficult shift. We can keep an eye on the corridor from the common room. Besides, we will only be ten minutes."

"You've convinced me. Tell you what, though. We could grab a takeaway and sit outside in sunshine. The fresh air will do us both good."

"Good idea," Stan said, opening the door to the discharge lounge.

"Do you think we need to lock the door?" Josie, said.

"Don't be silly. This door stays open day and night, twenty-four, seven," he said, closing it behind them and pausing to run his finger across the word: 'Mortuary' stamped in the middle of the door in bold, black letters.

"I can understand why we refer to the mortuary as the discharge lounge, can't you? Stan, said. "At the end of the day, discharge lounge is far easier on the ear and heart than the word mortuary. Then again, if patients overhear staff talking about the discharge lounge it doesn't have the same impact on them as the word mortuary would, does it?"

"You are right, Stan, the discharge lounge is far easier on the ear and heart of everyone. Mortuary and its connotations sound morbid, but, then again, someone has to work in there. It's a very important department. Let's get that drink and sit outside, on the bench, shall we?" Josie, said.

The two resisted the temptation to hold hands and made their way to the common room, which was quiet for the time of day.

"Sit down and I'll get us a drink," Stan said, but, before he could do so, their attention was drawn to a local newsflash filling the television screen in a corner of the room. They both remained motionless, respectful, as the announcement, they were only too aware of, was made.

"We interrupt this programme with a news bulletin. We can now confirm the names of the people who tragically lost their lives in the fatal collision on the A500 this morning, as:

Frederick Rindheart; a decorated, military hero.
Penelope Smithson; a figurehead for local charities.
Clarissa Noble and baby, of no fixed abode, and
Sarah Worth, a former government employee.

Weather and driving conditions continue to improve and we are pleased to report that the A500 is clear of debris. Our thoughts are with the families and friends of those who lost their lives in this morning's fatal road traffic accident."

Stan passed Josie a coffee in a cardboard cup and they walked, without saying a word, through the mortuary and the patio doors leading into the garden of remembrance.

Sitting together on their garden bench, Josie traced her finger across the plaque positioned in the centre of it.

Bench of Faith, Hope and Love
In memory of
Josie Woodridge and
Stanley Johnson
Who gave their lives fighting Covid
on this hospital's frontline

"I'm so grateful we were assigned to this place and time," Josie said, "because our work on earth was cut short by the pandemic."

"Me, too," Stan, said. "We hadn't finished our work here, had we? And, what could be more important than helping people to prepare for the journey of a lifetime by making their peace with each other and their maker?"

"Perhaps there is a morale in every one of their stories, Stan, not least our own," Josie, said. "We didn't really make hay while the sun was shining, did we? We always thought there would be tomorrow and missed too many opportunities to love and be loved." Stan didn't answer, but reached across the bench to hold her hand.

"We had better drink up, Josie, two more trollies have just arrived and, no doubt, we will soon have another story, or two, to tell," Stan, said.

Meanwhile, Fred, with Billy perched on his handlebars rode 'Fearless Sampson' into the sunset. Sarah boarded a heaven-bound train, cradling a baby boy in her arms. Clarissa and her mother, pushed a pram through the gates of glory together and last, but not least, Penelope, riding on the back of Champion, holding Sophie in front of her, galloped along heaven's seashore, into eternity's sunset.

OTHER BOOKS
BY THE AUTHOR

BURIED TEARS

BURIED WORTH

BURIED SINS

HELL'S TREES OF HEAVEN

A TALE OF TWO FRIENDS

NO MORE RAINBOWS

SUNSHINE AND SHADOWS

Printed in Great Britain
by Amazon

37118105R00119